"Are you still sorry about missing dessert?"

Mitch's slow, sexy grin was a wicked challenge.

Sam shook her head. "That was twice as good with none of the calories."

"Good answer." He wrapped an afghan around her naked shoulders and looked down at her, all satisfied male. "Next time I'll make sure there's a bed."

She blinked up at him. "Next time?"

"I'm a confident guy."

"There can't be a next time." The problem with losing control and rational thought was that when both returned, everything came back into focus in a rush. Sam couldn't regret what they'd done, but...

Why did there always have to be a *but?*

Dear Reader,

Have you ever heard this expression—if you do what you've always done, you'll get what you've always got? It came to my attention in the ongoing struggle to maintain my weight and resonated with me, because at just under five feet tall, every pound is lurking, ready to attach to my thighs. But not doing what I'd always done meant my favorite chips, cookies and candy would be rare treats and not staples of my daily diet. Unfortunately, the expression "old habits die hard" is also true. Change is never easy. And the hero of *Expecting the Doctor's Baby* finds this especially true.

Dr. Mitch Tenney is a gifted emergency room doctor who cares too much. He has zero tolerance for waste and doesn't hesitate to call 'em like he sees 'em, be it about a patient or hospital employee on his trauma team. Because making nice is not his specialty, a management counseling company is hired to train him in conflict resolution techniques and save his job. Mitch agrees under protest until he meets sweet, sassy Samantha Ryan and wants her as his relationship coach—among other things.

Mitch Tenney and Sam Ryan were fun characters and getting them to talk to each other was never difficult. They remind me of a lyric from the song "Beauty and the Beast"—barely even friends, then somebody bends unexpectedly. That's what change for the better is all about. I hope you enjoy reading their story as much as I enjoyed writing it.

All the best,

Teresa Southwick

EXPECTING THE DOCTOR'S BABY

TERESA SOUTHWICK

SPECIAL EDITION

Published by Silhouette Books

America's Publisher of Contemporary Romance

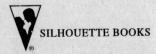

SILHOUETTE BOOKS

ISBN-13: 978-0-373-24924-4
ISBN-10:   0-373-24924-1

EXPECTING THE DOCTOR'S BABY

Copyright © 2008 by Teresa Ann Southwick

Visit Silhouette Books at www.eHarlequin.com

Printed in U.S.A.

Books by Teresa Southwick

Silhouette Special Edition

The Summer House #1510
   "Courting Cassandra"
Midnight, Moonlight &
   Miracles #1517
It Takes Three #1631
The Beauty Queen's Makeover #1699
At the Millionaire's Request #1769
§§*Paging Dr. Daddy* #1886
‡*The Millionaire and the M.D.* #1894
‡*When a Hero Comes Along* #1904
‡*Expecting the Doctor's Baby* #1924

Silhouette Books

The Fortunes of Texas:
Shotgun Vows

Silhouette Romance

Wedding Rings and
   Baby Things #1209
The Bachelor's Baby #1233
A Vow, a Ring, a Baby Swing #1349
The Way to a Cowboy's Heart #1383
And Then He Kissed Me #1405
With a Little T.L.C. #1421
The Acquired Bride #1474
Secret Ingredient: Love #1495
The Last Marchetti Bachelor #1513
**Crazy for Lovin' You* #1529
**This Kiss* #1541
**If You Don't Know by Now* #1560
**What If We Fall in Love?* #1572
Sky Full of Promise #1624
†*To Catch a Sheik* #1674
†*To Kiss a Sheik* #1686
†*To Wed a Sheik* #1696

††*Baby, Oh Baby* #1704
††*Flirting with the Boss* #1708
††*An Heiress on His*
   Doorstep #1712
§*That Touch of Pink* #1799
§*In Good Company* #1807
§*Something's Gotta Give* #1815

*The Marchetti Family
**Destiny, Texas
†Desert Brides
††If Wishes Were…
§Buy-a-Guy
‡The Men of Mercy Medical
§§The Wilder Family

TERESA SOUTHWICK

lives with her husband in Las Vegas, the city that
reinvents itself every day. An avid fan of romance
novels, she is delighted to be living out her dream of
writing for Silhouette Books.

I'd like to thank Marty Morrow and my husband, Tom, both dedicated health-care professionals who save lives every day. Your help on this project was invaluable. Thanks, guys.

Chapter One

He was getting ready to face death.

Samantha Ryan watched Dr. Mitch Tenney's expression change from bored and barely tolerant to fiercely intense when the call came in: drowning victim. ETA, five minutes.

He snapped out orders to the nurses behind the desk. "Page everyone. Get the trauma team down here. Paramedics are rolling with a kid. Pulled out of a pool. Not breathing. They've got an airway but couldn't get an IV. That means we need a cut-down tray. Get the crash cart and intubation tray—everything open and ready to go. I want respiratory and a ventilator. And the lab. We'll need blood gases stat." Intensity simmered in his dark blue eyes as he leveled a glare at everyone within glaring distance. "Move, people. This kid is two years old."

Sam felt her heart catch, followed by an adrenaline spike as he moved in her direction. She wanted to jump into action and do something even though she had no useful medical skills whatsoever. Besides, he hadn't been talking to her. She was there to observe him. Her job was to shadow him and take notes.

The E.R. manager had been notified that someone from Marshall Management Consultants would be there, and she had a temporary badge that kept her from being thrown out by security. But Dr. Tenney hadn't acknowledged her until now when he brushed past and ordered her to get the hell out of his way. She felt less useful than the fern at the nurses' station and just about as noticeable. But everyone noticed the dynamic doctor. Partly because of his looks.

The man could get work as a model or movie star if he walked away from medicine. Unlikely, since by all accounts he was brilliant—followed closely by the adjectives *abrasive, condescending* and *belligerent*. There were more, but those were the top vote-getters that were fit to print. He'd ticked off one too many people and his job here at Mercy Medical Center was in jeopardy. Her consulting company had been hired to salvage it with an attitude intervention ordered by his medical group and hospital administration.

Then the double doors whooshed open. Sam pressed her back into the wall, making herself as small as possible to keep out of the way as paramedics wheeled in a gurney and updated the E.R. staff. They rattled off numbers and words that didn't mean anything to her. The child was secured to a back board and a paramedic beside him was intermittently squeezing a bag. Sam had seen enough *E.R.* episodes to know that was to help him breathe. Mostly all she could see was matted brown hair that framed an impossibly small, frighteningly pale face. Then the glass doors closed off the trauma room and the child was surrounded by the platoon of professionals, led by Dr. Tenney, in the battle for his life.

Everyone was in blue scrubs and she had no idea who was who except Mitch. She couldn't hear anything, but it was like E. F. Hutton on crack. When he talked, they didn't just listen, someone jumped into action.

Sam wasn't sure how much time passed before he came out. And with staff still surrounding him, she couldn't see the boy.

Mitch walked up to the desk. "Is the family here yet, Rhonda?"

The buxom, blond E.R. nurse/manager looked up. "Mom's on the way, stuck in traffic on the Fifteen coming across the Strip. The teenage brother's here. He was babysitting."

Mitch's already grim expression tightened more as he nodded. "Okay."

Sam followed him through the double doors that separated the E.R. waiting area from trauma rooms. The brother wasn't hard to identify. He was the one in wet jeans and a white T-shirt with elbows braced on his knees and head bowed. He had a light blanket draped around his hunched shoulders. When she saw the doctor, the teenage girl beside him put her hand on his arm and he looked up.

He stood when Mitch stopped in front of him, feet set wide. There was another battle looming. Sam didn't want to see it, but she had no choice. Part of the reason she was here was to see how the doctor handled confrontation, then her boss could work out strategies to help him change the offending behavior. She moved off to the side where she could observe without being intrusive.

"How's my brother?"

"I stabilized him and he's on a ventilator to help him breathe."

"Is he going to be okay?"

"Looks like it. The paramedics got to him in time."

"I pulled him out of the pool."

The teenage girl moved beside him. "He did CPR. I called 9-1-1."

"Notify the mayor," Mitch snapped. "They'll throw a parade in your honor."

"What's your problem?" she demanded.

Mitch studied both teens before saying, "What are you on?"

"Nothing, dude." The boy looked away and shuffled his feet.

Sam knew the doctor was right when the kid didn't even ask what he meant. Drugs were involved in whatever happened.

"Right. Your pupils always look that big when the sun's up," Mitch said sarcastically. "Your brother had no head or body trauma. What happened to him?"

"Ty was there one minute, then he was gone."

"Basic common sense. You never turn your back on a child, especially near a pool."

"We didn't do anything."

"You can say that again."

"Lighten up." The boy pushed shaky fingers through hair the same shade as his brother's, but wouldn't look up.

"Reactions sluggish. What were you smoking? Grass? Crack?" When they started to protest Mitch cut them off with a curt, "Sell it somewhere else. It's my job to know this stuff. And I'm really good at my job. So are the cops. They're on the way."

"Cops? What for? We just went inside for a minute—the phone rang," she defended.

"It takes two to answer it?" He shook his head as he fisted his hands on his hips. "Even if I believed you, no phone call is so damn important that you had to take your eyes off a two-year-old by a pool. Ever."

"Hold on, dude—"

"Don't call me 'dude.' It's 'doctor' to you. And you hold on. Think about this. That child should be playing with toys and watching cartoons." He pointed an accusing finger at both of them. "You were supposed to protect him. You screwed up."

"But you said he'll be okay," the girl said, looking less defiant.

"We'll get an EEG to make sure. And he's still at risk for the next thirty-six to forty-eight hours. I want to know when his mother gets here." He glared at them one more time, then shook his head and disappeared back through the doors.

Sam let out a long breath. So that was the infamous Mitch Tenney in action, she thought. The hospital had a "three strikes and you're out" policy. Two complaints had already been filed and she may have just witnessed number three. It was a lousy situation and she was on his side, but he'd have been wiser to keep his opinions to himself and let the police handle it.

It was a relief that Darlyn Marshall, her boss, would be Mitch Tenney's counselor of record. Sam was a newbie at the up-and-coming company and he was the first client from Mercy Medical. With over two thousand hospital employees, it could be a lucrative contract. She didn't want to be responsible for blowing the situation because she had a mild case of hero worship.

He'd cheated death. In less gifted hands that child might not have been saved. Now it was up to Marshall Management Consultants to save *him*.

Mitch looked at the name plate on her desk—Samantha Ryan. He remembered her from the E.R., the day he'd worked on the kid, the drowning victim he'd almost lost. The memory tightened and twisted inside him. Stuff happened. He knew that. But some stuff didn't have to happen and his tolerance for stupidity was at an all-time low.

He met her gaze. Somehow the name fit her. Samantha—Sam—had sun-streaked brown hair and warm brown eyes that oozed optimism. When his gaze lowered to her mouth, a shot of lust went straight through him. Somewhere he'd heard the term "Cupid's bow" to describe a woman's mouth and he'd never quite gotten what that meant. Until now. Until looking at Sam Ryan.

He had the most absurd desire to see what her Cupid's bow mouth felt like, tasted like. If it was half as good and sweet as he was imagining, it could be a kiss of biblical proportions. Since *biblical* and *kiss* smacked of being an oxymoron, he figured his attention could be better concentrated elsewhere. Like messing with Ms. Ryan.

Or continuing to mess with her head. He'd just walked into her office and they'd been staring at each other across her desk, and the moment was stretching into awkward territory. He and *awkward* were old friends so he could keep it up indefinitely. But she looked tense and ill at ease. The question was how long before she folded under the pressure of needing to fill the silence with words. When she cleared her throat and swallowed, then shifted in her chair, he knew the wait was almost over.

"So, Dr. Tenney—"

"Call me Mitch."

She hesitated, then said, "Would you be more comfortable if I do?"

"Do you really care whether or not I'm comfortable?"

"Are you always so challenging?"

He folded his arms over his chest and looked down at her. "You think this is challenging?"

"I'm simply trying to learn more about you and your management style."

"Is that so?"

One corner of that fantasy mouth curved up. "If you insist on answering every question with a question, this process could be less productive than everyone hopes."

Good. *Everyone* was wasting his time. This appointment had been scheduled with top consultant Darlyn Marshall, but apparently she'd gone home sick. That worked for him. He didn't want to be here anyway, but the receptionist had shown him into this office. Looking at Sam Ryan was a hell of an entertaining way to spend this waste of time.

If he had to guess, he'd say she didn't share his sentiment. The phrase *acutely uncomfortable* came to mind and she was doing her level best not to show it.

"Have you been in the executive coaching business long, Ms. Ryan?"

"Why don't you call me Samantha?"

The question made him want to smile, but he held back. He suspected she was pretty green at this whole consulting thing, but she caught on to the game quick.

"How about Sam?" he asked.

"Would you be more comfortable with that?"

"Yes."

"Then Sam it is. Won't you sit down?" She held out her hand and indicated the chair in front of her desk.

"Thank you," he said politely. Politeness would confuse her, he thought. He wasn't sure why he felt the need to be a son of a bitch, but that's the way it was.

He glanced around the small office, located in a large building on Horizon Ridge Parkway, which was practically around the corner from Mercy Medical Center. There was no window in this glorified cubicle. She had an L-shaped desk with a computer to her right and a spindly tree struggling to survive in a pot in the corner. Mahogany frames lined the walls, but instead of pictures they contained motivational sayings. One boldly proclaimed Success is the Intelligent Use of Mistakes.

He couldn't afford to make mistakes. If he did someone died. Beside it was another one that read Obstacles Are Those Frightful Things You See When You Take Your Eyes Off Your Goals.

His goals weren't that complicated. Keep patients alive and don't get personal—with patients or anyone else. It worked for him.

On the wall behind her was a large picture of a suspension bridge at sundown. Underneath were the words Be a Bridge. Problems Become Opportunities When the Right People Join Together.

She looked up and saw him studying the print. "What do you think about that?"

He was going to hell for sure, but the kind of joining he imagined when he looked at her mouth had nothing to do with success in the workplace.

He shrugged. "It's a swell idea with no relevance in the real world."

"I'm glad to see you've come here with a completely open mind. How's that working for you?"

"Sarcasm," he said. "I like that in a woman."

Her lips pressed tight for a moment and she pulled nervously at the gold turtleneck sweater beneath her suede blazer. Her eyes now could only be described as brown because the optimism switch was turned off. He must have touched a major nerve.

"It's irrelevant whether or not you like me, Mitch. You need to focus on the goal."

"If keeping my eyes on you will get me there, I'm all for it."

When he grinned, she shifted her gaze from his and picked up a pair of black, square-framed glasses. After settling them on her nose she glanced at the paperwork in front of her. "All right then. Do you know why you're here?"

"Yes."

"Care to elaborate?"

"No."

Her lips compressed for a moment before she asked, "Are you familiar with the hospital's three-strikes policy?"

"You mean the one where it's three strikes and you're out? As in don't let the door hit you in the backside when you leave the building?"

She nodded. "That would be the one, yes."

"I'm familiar with it."

"Are you aware that you're halfway out that door and it's just about to…" Her gaze lowered and if his back was turned, he knew what part of his anatomy she'd be looking at. Her cheeks flushed pink. "Hit you in the hiney."

The blush made his view even better. This was starting to be less a waste of time and more fun by the minute. "Why, Ms. Ryan—Sam—I'm shocked and appalled. Is *hiney* official consulting terminology?"

"You're the doctor, Doctor. Is it the anatomically correct term for 'if you don't start taking this seriously your ass is grass'?"

He laughed. "Touché."

"The thing is you have two strikes. But you're in a class by yourself because you have two strikes in two different categories—patient complaints and employee complaints." She removed her glasses and met his gaze. "You already know that because your signature is on the paperwork, a clear indication that you've been apprised of the deep doo-doo you're in."

"Tough talk, Sam."

She shrugged. "It seems the only way to get your attention."

"You've got it." And how. She was beautiful and smart, a dynamite combination. "Now that you've got me what are you going to do with me?"

"Save your job."

"As goals go, it's a good one," he agreed.

"You remember me from the hospital," she reminded him. "It was my job to observe you."

"I see."

"The little boy who almost drowned? I'd like to talk about how you handled his caregiver."

His hands, resting flat on his thighs, curled into fists. "You mean the teenager who was so high his kid brother nearly died?"

"Unless you had results of a drug test, that was a guess on your part."

"*Educated* guess." He'd seen more than his share in the E.R. And he'd found his own brother high so many times recognizing drugged-out was second nature to him.

"Still, you didn't know for sure."

Yeah, he did. But this wasn't a hill he planned to die on. "What's your point?"

"The E.R. waiting room was full of people. Very public. Do you think that discussion would have been better conducted in private?"

Was she kidding? He'd just put a tube down a two-year-old's throat and hooked him up to a ventilator to breathe for him. Then he stood by while they checked electrical activity in his brain to see whether or not he'd be a vegetable for the rest of his life. In this case he wouldn't be, no thanks to the brother. Did he think? Hell, no. He'd reacted.

"I was updating the family on the patient's condition."

Her right eyebrow rose. "Is it possible that you were venting frustration? Perhaps less diplomatic than you could have been? Might you have been better off waiting for the police? And the boy's mother?"

Again with the questions designed to make him see the light. She might catch on quick, but she was still new at the game. He'd been doing it a lot longer.

"So, did you have a good time in the E.R.?" he asked.

"I tried to stay out of the way," she hedged. "I didn't want to be noticeable."

"Then you failed miserably. You're pretty hard to miss, Sam."

"You're saying I didn't blend?"

"Not even a little. The nurses were talking."

"Really?"

Her way of asking what they said. "On a scale of one to ten, they said you're a fifteen."

Actually, that was his scale, his assessment. His secret.

"Thank you."

He shrugged. "Just stating the obvious."

"No. You're changing the subject."

"Trying." He leaned back in his chair. "Nothing succeeds like the truth. And it worked for a minute there."

She referred to her notes. "Back on task—"

"Speaking of that. What are you doing for dinner tonight?"

When she met his gaze, her expression was wry. "I was planning to eat."

"By yourself?"

"Yes."

"Would you like company?"

"No."

"You sure?"

"Very." She shuffled the papers. "Now, as I was saying. After the trauma—"

She was kind of a pit bull. A pretty one. He was telling the truth about that scale thing. But apparently she wasn't going to let him distract her. "What about it?"

"First it should be acknowledged that there was a positive outcome."

"Yeah. The kid's alive, no thanks to his brother." Every

time he thought about what could have happened he wanted to put his fist through a wall. That kid was a baby and should never have had to go through something like that. No matter how young when it occurred, trauma changed a person. He should know. Trauma was his middle name, and not just because it was his job.

"Life is about as positive as it gets," he said.

"And it's thanks to you."

"And a lot of other people," he said.

"Absolutely. Thank you for bringing that up. Saving lives is a cooperative effort."

He'd given her the segue and she ran with it. Really smart girl. This was where she gave him the pitch for harmony equals effectiveness in a group situation. He had news for her.

"Have you ever been in a life-and-death situation, Sam?"

"Everyone struggles with issues—"

"Don't give me that touchy/feely crap. I'm talking about bleeding out, last breath, heart's got one beat left kind of trauma. Have you ever seen that?"

"No." She shifted in her chair.

"Then don't tell me that 'please and thank you' get the job done. It's messy in the trenches. You study, go through the training until gut instinct takes over and reaction is automatic. After that you keep your head up and focus. Sometimes even all of that's not enough."

She swallowed. "You cheat death."

"Every damn day. Every chance I get." He couldn't believe *she* got it.

"But you're here to talk about what happens when the trauma's over," she reminded him.

"You wait for the next one. You hold your breath for the next person who comes in because of something stupid. The car accident involving multiple vehicles because someone was text messaging. Or changing the radio. Spilled hot coffee—" He stopped, clenching his jaw. "Then the shift is over."

"I can see there's a lot of room for discussion. But speaking of over…" She looked at her watch. "Time's up, doctor—Mitch."

"It flies when you're having fun."

And he had. Mostly. Which was the surprise of the century. In his experience good surprises were few and far between. "So when can we do this again?"

"Stop at the front desk on your way out to make an appointment. Darlyn should be back in the office in a day or so. You can schedule your next meeting with her."

"What if I don't want to?"

She leaned forward and folded her hands on her desk. "You don't have a choice, Mitch. It's either executive coaching or administrative leave followed by door hitting hiney."

"So there is a choice."

"Have it your way."

"I usually do," he said.

She looked at him and her eyes widened as if she was on his wavelength. "In the unlikely event you're implying what I think you are, I need to make my position clear. Now that we've talked one on one, I'm absolutely certain that we wouldn't be a good professional fit."

He stood and rested a hip on the desk, satisfaction settling in when she leaned backward in the chair. It was a subtle movement, but definitely away from him without actually running for the hills.

"I couldn't disagree more, Sam. It's my professional opinion as a doctor, but more importantly as a man, that you and I would be an exceptionally good fit. I think I should have some say in who my coach is."

"That decision has already been made."

"Not by me." He had a pretty good idea what she saw in his face and didn't care. "You're the one I want."

Chapter Two

"What did you do wrong, Samantha?"

Sam fidgeted from one spiked heel to the other as she stood in front of her father's desk. She'd been summoned to his office at Mercy Medical Center to defend herself. It didn't matter that she was a grown woman, she felt like that motherless six-year-old again.

"I promise you I did nothing to undermine the relationship, Dad."

Unless she'd violated some unwritten Arnold Ryan moral code because she wasn't woman enough to make her fiancé want her more than that woman she'd caught him boinking. Unlike Mitch Tenney, who had said out loud and with great determination and conviction that he *did* want her.

The memory sent a shiver of lust skidding through her, which was worse than stupid because he'd meant he wanted her to be his relationship coach. And he only said that because he thought she was an inexperienced pushover who would give him credit for the time without making him do any of the work. Because he was too close to the mark for comfort, she'd stubborned up and refused his request. He hadn't been a happy client when he'd left her office yesterday.

Her father cleared his throat. Loudly. "Samantha? Are you paying attention to me?"

Sam started. "Of course, Dad."

Arnold Ryan was the hospital's administrator and chief executive officer. In his late fifties, he was still strikingly handsome, tall and fit, with ice-blue eyes and silver-streaked black hair. The man who'd run out on her mother before Sam was old enough to remember had never been more than a sperm donor. The one sitting behind his desk in the office where he managed the largest hospital corporation in Las Vegas was the only father she'd ever known. She was still trying her best to make him proud of her. That's why she'd come running on her lunch hour.

"I had to find out from Jax that the two of you are no longer engaged to be married. And haven't been for several weeks."

Subtext: once again she'd messed up. It was too much to hope she could avoid this scene. How to put a positive spin on procrastinating. "You're involved with union negotiations, Dad, and I didn't want to distract you. I was waiting for the right time."

"When a decision is bad, there is no right time. He's an up-and-comer in the hospital corporation. You could do worse. What is the problem, Samantha? Why did you break off the engagement?"

How did she phrase this to avoid telling him that Jax Warner, the man her father had enthusiastically endorsed, was not the man of her dreams? "It was a mutual, amicable decision," she said.

"That tells me absolutely nothing." Her father rested his elbows on his desk and steepled his fingers as he nailed her with a look.

She plucked nonexistent lint from her navy blue skirt, then tugged the hem of the matching jacket to smooth the line. Since he'd handpicked the man, there was no way she'd tell him the whole truth. Somehow he would twist it around and make it her fault.

What she needed was a distraction, something positive to take his mind off the broken engagement. "I can tell you that my company snagged the hospital's employee counseling contract."

He glanced up and irony mixed with disdain in his expression. "I had nothing to do with that decision."

"Of course not," she protested. "That's not what I was implying. The triumph is all the sweeter because Marshall Management Consultants obtained it entirely on merit."

"I was against designating any funds for something so frivolous, but the director of human resources felt it was important to salvage employees in a personnel-scarce market."

"It's a good decision, Dad. We can help—"

"Oh?" One jet-black eyebrow rose as a sardonic expression suffused his face. "Face it, Samantha. You couldn't save your engagement. It's time you got a real job." He pointed at her. "Or, better yet, do a better job. *Be* a relationship coach. Apologize for whatever you did to Jax. I'm certain he'll forgive you and the wedding will be back on."

Shoots and scores, Sam thought. Sometimes she forgot that lectures were best endured silently. Any attempt at conversation simply tacked on an opportunity for him to make her feel more inadequate. Thirty minutes later, after her father reminded her again of the time he would pick her up for the hospital's fund-raiser on Saturday at Caesar's Palace, she left the office.

"There should be an expectation of fidelity in an engagement," she muttered, marching down the hall in a haze of anger. "What am I, thirteen? He should not quit his day job to be a matchmaker. Dr. Phil couldn't salvage that jerk—"

"Sam—"

Some part of her brain registered the familiar, deep voice,

but a larger part was still focused on her hostility. "How is this my fault? What is this? The Middle Ages—"

"Hey, Sunshine. Who rained on your parade?"

She stopped and turned. Mitch Tenney stood just behind her in the hall, leaning a shoulder against the wall, arms folded over an impressively broad chest. Stubble darkened his jaw in the sexiest possible way and the spark of humor in his eyes enhanced the effect. Not to mention that he certainly knew how to fill out a pair of blue scrubs. How could that be? They were shapeless cotton with a drawstring in the pants—glorified pajamas—but he made them look *good*. The sight of Mercy Medical's resident troublemaker sent a jolt through her like she'd never felt from Jax the jerk.

"Mitch. What are you doing here?"

"I work here."

She smacked her forehead. "Right. The pajamas were a clue."

"Pajamas?" One corner of his mouth curved up.

"I meant scrubs." If only the earth would open and swallow her whole.

"What's your excuse?" he asked. "For being here, I mean."

"You don't want to know."

"Okay. But a word to the wise. If you're not careful, trash-talking in the hall will get you sent to the principal's office for detention."

If he was one of the bad boys she'd get to hang out with it would be worth the risk. As opposed to the unacceptable risk of counseling him. Her reaction just now was proof that her female instincts were firing on all cylinders. She was far too attracted, which cancelled out her objectivity, making it impossible for her to work with him.

"Thanks for the advice. See you around." She started to walk away.

"Wait."

She sighed and turned back. "What?"

"Have lunch with me." He cocked a thumb over his shoulder. "I'm on my way to the doctors' dining room."

"I don't think that's a good idea."

"Have you already eaten?"

She'd eaten crow in her father's office, but that's not what he meant. "I'll grab a bite on the way back to the office."

"I'm buying," he offered.

"Correct me if I'm wrong, but doctors don't pay. Hence the name, doctors' dining room. Free food is a perk. I don't belong."

She settled the strap of her purse more securely on her shoulder, wincing at how pathetic that sounded. But he knew nothing about her and had no reason to paint her words with the pity brush.

"I can get you in. If you're with me no one will question you." He angled his head in that direction. "The food is pretty good."

"It doesn't feel right—" For so many reasons, not the least of which was professional.

"Haven't you ever wanted to throw caution to the wind and break the rules?"

Not until now, she thought. "It never works for a girl like me. We always get caught."

"Live dangerously."

Just standing here this close to him felt dangerous. Sam didn't want to think about the fallout of sharing a meal with him. "Mitch, I really don't think I should—"

He held up his hand. "Before you finish that statement, you should know that I don't take no for an answer."

Was he talking about lunch? Or her refusal to be his counselor? Because if that was what he meant, he was doomed to disappointment.

"Sometimes we don't have a choice," she said.

"Maybe. But now isn't one of those times. Have lunch with me, Sam." He grinned, then took her arm and guided her down the hall. "Another happy by-product of being with me is that no one can accuse you of talking to yourself."

He really didn't take no for an answer, she thought, letting him lead her into the dining room. The smell of food assaulted her and made her stomach growl. She'd entered the inner sanctum.

"So this is where they feed the medical gods," she said.

"Pretty impressive, huh?"

She looked around at groupings of tables covered with white cloths, matching napkins and tweed chairs scattered throughout the room. There was a steam table for hot food and a cold one filled with greens, fruits and creamy-based salads. Waiters in white jackets delivered drinks to several people, then cleared used plates.

Sam glanced up at him. "I've been to the cafeteria and we're definitely not in Kansas anymore."

"Stick with me, Sunshine. I'll take you to all the good places."

Following Mitch's example she picked up a tray, plate and utensils then chose small portions of seafood, salad, fruit and a sugar cookie for dessert. On second thought, she picked up another one because she needed the comfort food after seeing her father. The room was still nearly empty but Mitch headed for a quiet spot in the far corner and she followed him.

After settling, the waiter walked over and took their drink orders—coffee for him, iced tea for her. When the liquids were delivered, they ate in silence for a few moments. Because of a deeply ingrained personal aversion to long silences, Sam felt the need to fill this one.

"So you're working today?" she asked.

"What was your first clue?"

"The fact that you're here, for one. And dressed in scrubs. That's two clues. Have you been busy?"

"You mean have I offended anyone today?" he asked.

"I actually didn't mean that, but... Have you?"

He shook his head. "It's clear, however, that someone offended you."

"What was *your* first clue?" She put down her fork and picked up a cookie.

"Besides looking like you wanted to rip someone's head off?" He sipped his coffee. Black. "So, who's the jerk?"

"I have to pick one?" she asked.

His eyebrows rose as he set his cup back on the saucer. "A plethora of jerks? You are having a bad day. Tell me about it."

There was no reason not to and it would fill that pesky silence. "For starters there's my fiancé—ex-fiancé," she amended.

"What did he do to become an ex?"

"I found him in bed with someone he wasn't engaged to." She chewed thoughtfully. "Although they *were* engaged in— Never mind."

"That definitely qualifies him for jerk status."

"Not according to my father. Stepfather, actually," she clarified.

"Did you tell him the jerk cheated on you?"

She picked up cookie number two. "Not exactly."

"What exactly did you tell him?"

"That we had a mutual parting of the ways." She saw his skeptical expression and hurriedly added, "It was just easier than the truth. I didn't want to make Dad feel bad. He introduced us and thought we'd be the perfect couple."

"And what did Arnie say?" he asked, the sarcastic tone hinting at his less than positive opinion of her father.

"He said that I should try to patch things up. After that he indicated that if I was any good at what I do, I could salvage the relationship. For thirty minutes I silently listened to how inadequate I am. How I should get a real job. Something I'm good at. If I can't do that, then finding a man to marry me—make that take care of me—would be the best solution."

"That would imply you're a problem."

She shrugged. "It's just that he doesn't have a lot of respect for my profession or just about anything else I do, for that matter."

"You're kidding, right?" Mitch stared at her.

"If only."

And now that her pity party was over she wanted the invitation back. It wasn't her habit to talk to a relative stranger, not to mention a client of her firm, about her personal problems. She could only blame anger and a healthy dose of nerves for spilling her guts like that. Mitch Tenney made her nervous in a stomach-fluttering, weak-knees kind of way. And he used silence like a scalpel to open her up. She'd felt an obsessive need to put words in the void and said whatever came to mind. Since she'd just seen her father, all that stuff came out of her mouth.

Mitch's fork clattered on the plate and he stared at her. "I'm waiting for the part where you told the arrogant ass to take a flying leap. And I mean Arnie, not the ex."

"You'd be waiting for a long time." She sighed.

"You didn't say anything."

How could she explain this to a man who was so straightforward he said what was on his mind and let the chips fall anywhere? "My father isn't perfect."

"You can say that again." He stared at her. "It seems to me

you dodged a bullet with the ex and father jerk should be doing the dance of joy instead of calling you on the carpet."

Her heart did a fluttery, pounding thing in her chest. He barely knew her, yet he was on her side. It was new; it was nice. But Mitch was reacting to what she'd told him in anger. It wasn't the whole truth.

"Arnold Ryan is the only father I've ever known. He adopted me and, after my mother died, he raised me with his own children. I don't know what I'd have done without him. He's my family and he's been good to me."

"Define *good to you.* Because from where I'm sitting putting down your profession and ordering you to apologize to a cheater who doesn't deserve you doesn't sound like *good.*"

"When you put it like that, it sounds—"

"Way wrong?"

Yes, but she wouldn't admit that. "My father said what he did because he wants what's best for me," she explained.

"Put-downs, recriminations and bad advice?" Mitch met her gaze. "How's that working for you?"

When he said it like that, not so well. It made her a hypocrite who coached others to confront conflict in a productive way when she couldn't follow the same advice. It made her a do-as-I-say-not-as-I-do kind of person.

It made her a doormat. A man like Mitch had no use for a doormat. There was no reason on earth she should care whether or not he had a use for her, but she did.

"Mitch? Are you paying attention?"

He looked up from the doodles on his legal pad and found his partners' attention fixed on him. Dr. Jake Andrews and Dr. Cal Westen were his best friends. The three of them had done their residency in trauma medicine at the county hospital in

Las Vegas. Rumor had it they were known as the axis of attraction as well as the trifecta of heart trauma.

After completing training, they decided to open the group and contract with Mercy Medical Center to provide trauma specialists for the E.R. In this small office they had a clerical staff for billing and conducted monthly status meetings. This was one of those and his presence had been mandatory, but no one had said anything about paying attention.

"Sorry. My mind was wandering." He'd been distracted by a pair of brown eyes that were several units low on optimism.

"Listen up." Six-foot-tall, dark-haired, gray-eyed Jake had taken on the business side of the practice and fell into the role of leader. "You're on the agenda."

"Oh?"

"Don't play dumb." Cal folded his arms on the table. His sandy hair and blue eyes gave him a boyish look. It attracted women in droves, the ones who didn't know about or were misguided enough to believe they could change his love-'em-and-leave-'em style. "You got the memo about today's topics. You're on it."

"Okay. Let's go."

Cal held up his hand. "This isn't a barroom brawl we're taking into the alley. It's a medical practice."

"What's your point?" Mitch asked.

"I'll get to it. When it's time."

"I think it's time now." Mitch sat up straight and looked across the mahogany table at his partners. This felt a lot like an ambush.

Jake met his gaze for several moments, then finally nodded. "No reason we can't take it out of order. Let's talk about what's going on with you."

"I'm doing great."

"I meant the mandated counseling," Jake clarified.

"About that," Mitch said. "Can we discuss why you guys threw me under the bus and jumped in bed with that HR guy at the hospital?"

"Yeah," Cal said. "We can start with why you reprimanded a nurse simply for doing her job."

"If that were the case," Mitch said, "I probably wouldn't have said anything."

"You got on her case for not hanging an IV fast enough," Cal said. "Her complaint states that the E.R. was nuts and she was following her training to triage doctor's orders."

"The problem was it never got done and someone who came in for help fell through the cracks," Mitch defended. "I don't write orders unless they're important and if I write it, I want it done."

"The incident is under review with the E.R. director and human resources. If she files a grievance with the union, in addition to patient complaints about your abusive attitude, there will be hell to pay."

"That's part of my specialty," Mitch said.

He'd shaken hands with the devil more than once. It held no fear for him.

Cal shook his head in exasperation. "That's just one of a laundry list from the hospital staff. Now let's talk about how you told off a doctor."

Mitch remembered the incident. The guy blew off his patient's symptoms during an office appointment forcing an E.R. visit that made the situation more traumatic than it should have been. "He didn't do his job."

"It's not your job to make that judgment—especially in front of the patient." Jake's voice was lower than normal, meaning he was ticked off. "There are numerous ways to handle something like that."

Sam had said something similar. He liked it better coming from her. "I didn't think it could wait."

"The bottom line is that you didn't think," Jake snapped. "This guy is threatening to go to the medical executive committee. If he pushes for a peer review we could be in a world of hurt."

"If it goes that far I'll get to tell my side. There won't be a problem," Mitch soothed.

"Look, Mitch," Cal said, his tone conciliatory, "we just have to do damage control. Your counseling is part of it. You need to be tolerant—"

"Not happening. I never understand losing a patient." Mitch had seen too much of stupidity, indifference and playing the game. Too much life thrown away. He'd had it up to here with keeping his mouth shut. "I call that a waste."

"We all feel that way," Jake said. "But Mercy Medical is expanding. They're getting ready to break ground on a new campus with a level-two trauma center. Our contract is up soon. We need to renegotiate and we're talking a lot of money. This is the worst possible time for an incident. You have to demonstrate a willingness to learn how to play nice with others."

The only person he'd met that he wanted to play nice with was Sam Ryan, and she'd refused to play at all.

"How's the relationship counseling going?" Cal asked, a little too close to the mark.

"I think it's a waste of time."

"Good attitude," Jake said.

Mitch shrugged. "I'm not in to that touchy/feely stuff."

"Your style is more shoot-from-the-hip," Jake agreed. "Consider this people skills triage."

"And what if I don't?" Mitch asked.

Cal's blue eyes were troubled. "We won't let you take down the whole practice."

"You're going to throw me out?" Mitch said.

"Let's not go there." Jake held up his hands, gesturing for peace. "Marshall Management Consultants comes highly recommended. You did keep the appointment?"

"Yeah."

"And?"

"It's too soon to say." Mitch leaned back in his chair.

He didn't want to get their hopes up because he was pretty sure no one could help him. He had the history to back up that assessment. He hadn't been a good brother, son, or husband. The opportunity to be a father had been ripped away from him without his say so and he'd never had the chance to try. He was only good at saying what was on his mind and being an E.R. doc.

"But I'll do my time," he agreed.

"Fair enough." Cal looked down at the notes in front of him. "Next item on the agenda—"

Mitch half listened to more specifics on expansion and hiring while the rest of his concentration was taken up with Sam Ryan. Doing his time would be more pleasant if he could spend it with her. When she'd said they wouldn't be a good fit, his thoughts had gone to where they were horizontal on the handiest flat surface and fitting together the way God intended a man and woman to fit. Running into her at the hospital earlier today had convinced him that his first impression had been dead on.

She was like sunshine on a cloudy day. When it's cold outside, she's the month of May. If Jake and Cal could hear his thoughts, they'd start humming the tune. But it was true.

In his opinion, her excuse for refusing to work with him was nothing more than spin for the fact that she didn't like him. There was a lot of that going around and he had a file full of grievances to prove it.

Except that didn't hold water considering the way she'd opened up to him about the run-in with her father. Would she have done that if she hated his guts? More to the point, why had he requested her counseling services in the first place?

Because he liked baiting her. He liked how her full mouth compressed when she was annoyed. He liked the way her brown eyes warmed when she was pleased. And he especially liked when she asked him if he'd offended anyone today. The prospect of working with her was more exciting than he would have thought when he'd been forced into it. When life gives you lemons, and all that…

"So Mitch will be representing us at the black-tie fund-raiser for the hospital," Cal said, interrupting his thoughts.

Mitch heard his name, fund-raiser and black tie—all of which got his attention. "Say again."

Cal grinned. "We paid twenty-five hundred dollars for the privilege of attending a fund-raising event put on by Mercy Medical Center at Caesar's Palace. You drew the short straw."

"Since when?" Mitch demanded.

"For one thing, it's your punishment for shooting your mouth off too many times," Jake answered. "And it's what you get for not paying attention just now."

That part was all Sam Ryan's fault, he thought. If he'd come up with a strategy to convince her to work with him, the punishment would have been worth it. All he'd gotten was monkey suit duty.

He'd have to bring up the matter the next time he saw her. And there would be a next time.

Chapter Three

"Samantha, you look beautiful tonight."

"Thanks, Dad."

The approval in her father's eyes was worth all the trouble and expense. She wanted him to be proud of her, but she was also representing Marshall Management tonight. Projecting an aura of professionalism and confidence required the right dress and she'd blown her budget on this stunner.

The white, one-shouldered, sequined Grecian gown hugged her body in a sophisticated, yet demure way. Silver high-heeled sandals and a small matching clutch bag completed her outfit. After she put highlights in her mousy brown hair, the stylist swept it away from her face and fashioned a bun of curls to the side, behind her ear. Silver eye shadow made her eyes look enormous and subtle body glitter made her exposed skin shimmer.

"You're pretty awesome yourself," she said, admiring how handsome and distinguished her father looked in his traditional black tuxedo.

He smiled down at her. "I have to meet some people for a drink. You'll be all right on your own?"

"Of course." She nodded. "I have to network, too."

"I'll see you later then."

She watched him disappear into the crowd of people

already gathered for cocktails in the reception area outside the room where dinner would be served. Several bars were set up and signs directed guests to a private corner displaying items donated for a silent auction. Sam had contributed three counseling sessions on behalf of Marshall Management.

Darlyn was supposed to be here, too, but was still not feeling well. She'd given Sam a list of contacts to touch base with and directed her to dazzle them with her charm. She wasn't sure about the charm part, but if she could find a particularly magnificent chandelier and stand under it, dazzling wouldn't be a problem.

There would be a lot of hospital management types here. Like her father, they were old school and skeptical about the benefits of corporate counseling. Her company had a foot in the door now, an opportunity to prove their services were money well spent. She spotted one of her must-sees. After snagging a glass of white wine from the tray of a circulating waiter, Sam wove her way through the crowd.

"Amanda Jones," she said. The tall, black-haired woman turned at the sound of her name. She was in her fifties and was the director of a large staff of physical therapists. Sam held out her hand. "Samantha Ryan."

The woman smiled. "From Marshall Management."

Sam nodded. "Darlyn wanted me to make it a point to say hello for her."

"She's not here?"

"No. Her cold is hanging on and she didn't want to spread the joy."

"And we're all grateful," Amanda said. "How long have you been with her?"

"About six months. I'm excited for the opportunity to work with Darlyn."

"She's very good at what she does. I understand she did some pretty fast talking and convinced the powers that be at Mercy Medical to send problematic employees in for counseling?"

Sam nodded. "I don't have to tell you how costly it is to train someone, then lose them when they're finally productive over something that could be avoided with intervention."

"Finding and retaining qualified personnel can also make a difference for the patients in an ongoing situation," Amanda agreed.

Sam took a sip of wine. "The hospital's human resources director was instrumental in securing the contract with Marshall Management."

And tonight was all about taking the connection out for a spin with the possibility of bringing in future business.

Her job was to put a face with a name and get it out there.

"How's that working out?" Amanda asked.

"I've had several sessions with one of the respiratory therapists who is wonderful with kids, but not so much the adults. She's very receptive to learning techniques to deal with conflict in a less confrontational manner."

"I see."

Sam glanced at the doorway and her heart stuttered when she recognized another high-profile and infamous client weaving his way through the crowd. Mitch Tenney was taller than most, so it wasn't difficult to spot him. Avoiding him was another issue entirely.

Part of her job was public relations and this was too public for Mitch to miss her unless she ducked behind a marble column and hid for the rest of the night.

"Amanda, it's been a pleasure talking with you. If you'll excuse me, there's someone over there I need to…" She pointed to a place on the opposite side of the room from where Mitch was standing.

"Thanks for the information, Sam. Good to meet you."

"You, too." Sam smiled then slid through the crowd of people. What the heck was *he* doing here?

But she knew the answer. This was a fund-raiser. The hospital had a mutually beneficial relationship with all the physicians who had privileges there. For all his flaws, her father had a noble goal and had put the pressure on everyone to make this fund-raiser a success. He was determined to build a cancer treatment center at Mercy Medical and dedicate it to the memory of her mother, who had died of the disease. He had loved her very much. It wasn't his fault he couldn't love her daughter.

Sam made her way to the other side of the room but couldn't shake the sensation of awareness. She felt like the princess and the pea—she couldn't see him but she *knew* he was there.

And then it happened. The crowd parted like the Red Sea and he spotted her. It was too much to hope he would simply wave and walk away. That wasn't the Tenney technique. He grinned and headed for her like a magnet to true north. His long legs put him in front of her before the static in her brain cleared.

"Sam, what a pleasant surprise."

"Hello." Clever comeback, she thought.

"And just like that, an evening I thought would be boring is anything but."

Based on what the sight of him in a tuxedo was doing to her insides, *boring* was the last word that came to her mind. The first word would be *sex* and if all his harnessed intensity was aimed at her, she'd be in his bed, no questions asked.

"So what brings you here?" he asked.

"I'm working, actually. Networking. Darlyn was supposed to be here also, but she's still under the weather. So I'm on my own representing the firm." She was babbling and took a sip of wine to stop herself. "How are you, Mitch?"

"Better now." His gaze boldly checked her out from head to toe. "You look amazing."

"Thanks." She decided to mimic his bold appraisal and looked him up and down. "You clean up pretty good yourself. Quite a change from the pajamas."

He glanced down. "Speaking of monkey suits... It's your fault I'm here."

How did she interpret that comment and respond appropriately? He didn't look annoyed. More like a predator on the prowl.

"Is that so?"

"Yeah. At our monthly status meeting my associates drafted me to represent them when I was preoccupied with figuring out how to convince you that we would work well together."

The glitter in his blue eyes made her heart hammer against the inside of her chest. Suddenly there wasn't enough air in the huge room, which made a witty comeback something of a challenge.

"Oh?"

"I promised myself that I'd bring it up the next time I saw you, but never expected I'd have the pleasure so soon." He took her elbow and steered her to the bar, where he ordered a Jack Daniel's on the rocks.

For someone who relied on talking to put food on the table and a roof over her head, being around Mitch was an incredibly humbling experience. Which was a good portion of the reason she could never work with him. She emptied her wineglass and set it on the bar.

"So, you don't like dressing up?" she said, watching him take his drink, then slip five dollars into the bartender's tip glass.

"I'm much more comfortable in my pajamas," he answered, a knowing glint in his eyes.

Warmth crept into her cheeks. As far as his attire went, the pajamas were a good look. But in black tie and jacket he was a tall, dark, handsome fantasy come to life. How could she not fantasize about being in his arms with his lips pressed to hers?

Good grief. She needed to get away. "It's nice to see you again. But if you'll excuse me, I'm going over there to check out the silent auction items."

"Great idea," he said, falling into step beside her.

The man couldn't take a hint if she pressed it into his hand. He was the perverse type who would stick like glue if she asked him to get lost. She simply turned away and felt his gaze on her as he followed.

They browsed the items on display—jewelry, paintings, pricey glass art, spa packages—and stopped by the large sign that read Marshall Management Consultants. After reading the fine print, he set his drink down and filled out a bid, then stuck it in the box.

"Wouldn't you rather have a picture or a weekend spa getaway?" she asked.

He drained the contents of his glass and the ice clinked when he lowered it. "No."

She folded her arms over her chest and blushed when the movement drew his gaze there. He made no effort to hide his positive reaction.

"Since when did you change your mind about what I do?"

"Since a very wise woman pointed out to me that if I don't, my ass could be grass and in jeopardy of getting hit by the door on my way out."

"You're already getting counseling sessions," she reminded him. "Why would you voluntarily buy more?"

"Let's just say that I always get what I want."

Sam didn't miss the expression in his eyes, the intensity snapping there. She got that familiar, fluttery sensation in the pit of her stomach because the look clearly said he wanted *her.* And not for counseling.

She had a feeling what he wanted didn't actually involve talking.

Mitch leaned back and slid his left arm across the back of Sam's chair, noting that his fingers literally itched from the urge to touch her shoulder and explore the shimmery, sexy, mysterious softness of her skin. He took a steadying breath and glanced around the ballroom, lights dimmed for dinner. Flower arrangements in fall colors of orange, gold and brown decorated the tables, garnished with small pumpkins as a salute to Halloween coming in a few weeks. Candles glowed from the center of the array and the flame only made his dinner companion look more captivating.

He leaned closer and said, "I told you to stick with me. Is this a good place, or what?"

"Technically I'm not with you," she said pleasantly. "My father gave me a ride. And you crashed this table."

"A gentleman wouldn't abandon a lady whose date is home sick. Especially a lady who looks so beautiful."

"Oh, please—"

He touched a finger to her lips, stopping the words, but kicking her pulse into a flutter. If he hadn't been focused on the fascinating place where clavicle and neck collided, he might have missed it. Tapping gently, he said, "Don't say anything you'll regret."

"I'd just like to say that if you insinuated yourself next to me in order to continue your campaign to change counselors, you're wasting your breath."

"The seat was open," he said, feigning self-righteous indignation. "I only wanted to keep you company."

"And I was looking at this as an opportunity to meet strangers."

"Problems become opportunities when the right people join together," he said, quoting the words on her wall.

"Exactly," she agreed.

"How about for tonight we call a truce? You won't ask if I've been playing well with others and I won't hit you up to be my coach." He held out his hand. "Deal?"

She looked at it, hesitating.

"What?" he asked, meeting her gaze.

"I'm just trying to find the asterisk in that statement."

He frowned. "I'm sorry?"

"You know, the asterisk. Have you ever noticed that everything has an asterisk—an exception to the rule? Fine print. Excluded under the warranty. Discount applies only when a pregnant ape swings across the freeway at exactly 12:01. Life is an asterisk and one always needs to tread carefully lest they rear up and bite one in the backside."

"I'm shocked and appalled," he said.

"Oh?"

"Who knew the poster girl for optimism, voted most likely to be positive, bright and cheery, had such a cynical side."

"Go figure."

Her shrug did amazing things to the bare shoulder that was driving him completely nuts.

"All I'm saying is that we agree not to talk shop," he clarified.

"Okay."

But before they could talk about anything, the public address system emitted static and then Arnold Ryan was introduced. Since their backs were to the dais, Sam turned her chair around to see. Mitch did the same and managed to get his close enough to brush her arm. The contact left a trail of silver glitter on the black sleeve of his jacket and he thought how characteristic of her to leave a glow on everything she touched.

"Good evening, ladies and gentlemen," Arnie greeted the crowd. "Thank you all for coming. We're gathered here for a cause near and dear to my heart."

That's when it hit Mitch that he'd been pressed into service because of being in the doghouse and hadn't bothered to get any details.

He leaned over to Sam and whispered, "Does he actually have a heart?"

She turned to look at him and their lips were inches apart. Her eyes widened a fraction before she said, "Of course he does."

"What is he talking about?"

"Did you bother to read your invitation?" she asked.

"No."

She shook her head in exasperation, but the corners of her mouth curved up as if she would expect this from him. "My father is kicking off a fund-raising drive for the Catherine Mary Ryan Cancer Center. Colon cancer killed my mother and he wants to fund a diagnosis-and-treatment facility dedicated to her memory."

"The valley certainly needs one." The dim light underscored the shadows in her eyes and he recalled her saying she'd been raised with Ryan's children. "How old were you when your mother died?"

"Six."

His father died because his cop instincts made him intervene in a convenience store robbery. Mitch knew how it felt to lose a parent at a young age, but he'd had his mother. And Robbie for a while. Senseless death made him angry. The guilt and pain that haunted him twisted together and knotted in his gut.

"Mitch?"

He blinked, clearing away visions of the past and focused on Sam. "That must have been tough. Losing your mom so young."

She nodded. "But every cloud has a silver lining and tonight is all about that. Making something good come out of tragedy."

In his opinion the two were mutually exclusive, but he wouldn't tell her that because the sparkle was back in her eyes. He wouldn't live up to her low expectations and say anything to snuff it out.

"That's the spirit, Sunshine."

Before she could respond to that, the room erupted in applause because her father had completed his remarks. Sam stood to turn her chair around and he took care of that like the chivalrous guy he was. When they sat again, he noticed the waitstaff was distributing dessert and coffee while a group of musicians set up behind the lectern at the front of the room.

"Looks like there's going to be dancing," he commented.

"On the invitation it was clearly stated that the evening included cocktail hour, dinner and dancing."

"I like surprises."

"See. Even boring clouds have a silver lining."

"Maybe. But only if you'll take a turn with me on the dance floor." He was sure she'd turn him down and was already marshaling his arguments.

"I'd love to," she said.

Strains of a slow song drifted to them and he stood, holding out his hand to her. She slid her fingers into his palm and when she rose, the muted light caught the sequins in her dress and the glitter on her skin.

Speaking of surprises... He'd get to hold the silver lining in his arms.

The wooden floor in the center of the room filled with other couples and Mitch placed Sam's hand in the crook of his arm as he led her there. He held his breath, anticipating the pleasure of her closeness. Then he pulled her into his arms and found the softness of her pressed against him more intoxicating than his Jack Daniel's.

He looked down at her. "I was sure you'd tell me to take a hike."

"I love to dance."

"So I could be any jerk off the street and you'd have agreed?"

Her alluring mouth curved up when she smiled. "I believe we established that my jerk quota has been filled recently. So, I'd have to say no."

"Then I'm not on your jerk list?"

"I don't think that about you. Quite the opposite."

He found her completely charming and was grateful to be on her good side. "What's the opposite of a jerk?"

"You're a guy who saves lives. In my book that makes you a—"

"Here you are, Samantha," said a voice behind them.

Sam leaned to the side. Even with heels she wasn't tall enough to see over his shoulder. "Hi, Dad."

Mitch turned and deliberately left his arm around Sam's waist. "Ryan."

"Dr. Tenney. How nice of you to join us this evening." His tone said he wasn't actually feeling the love.

"You throw a great party," Mitch answered politely, if only to prove to Sam that he could be polite.

"Thank you. The turnout is very gratifying." He looked at Sam. "My remarks were well received."

"Absolutely," she answered, tensing.

They'd been too busy talking to listen to the speech. In his opinion Arnold Ryan was a pompous ass who gave his daughter a hard time for no good reason. Mitch tightened his hand on her waist, hoping she felt his support.

"So, Doctor, how are things in the E.R.?" Ryan asked.

Mitch shrugged. "Funny you should ask. Sam was just singing my praises."

"Samantha is easily impressed," he said, with a sardonic look at his daughter.

"No," she said. "When I was there for his precounseling observation he saved a drowning victim the paramedics brought in. A little boy. Two years old."

Arnold slid his hands into the pockets of his tux trousers. "It's a good thing he was there."

The sarcasm in his tone told Mitch he was indeed one slipup away from the door hitting him in the backside on the way out. He wasn't sure why this guy disliked him, but the feeling was becoming more mutual by the minute.

"Dad, it was the most amazing thing to watch the E.R. staff work together to save that child."

"The E.R. staff is very good at what they do," Mitch informed her father. "They have to be because we see everything from car accidents to the common cold. But I don't have to tell you that."

"No, you don't."

"Mercy Medical is lucky to have a doctor with his skills," Sam said.

"And he definitely has them. Along with a finely tuned abrasive streak. If only rudeness saved lives," Ryan snapped.

"We're still dealing with the fallout from your confrontation after that particular incident."

"I hate waste," Mitch said, anger knotting in his gut. "Makes it hard to be diplomatic."

"That's where my profession comes in," Sam said quickly, looking very uncomfortable. "Smoothing out the rough edges will make him even better at what he does."

"What he does is take the rules and bend them into oblivion."

"Just give the counseling time, Dad. Darlyn Marshall is also very good at what she does. Sometimes people don't realize how they come across and simply need to learn coping techniques to keep the little things from turning into big issues."

"If I hold my breath waiting for that," her father said, "I would be in urgent need of emergency services myself. Either someone fits in or they don't. Talking it to death is an exercise in futility."

"You do realize you're referring to your daughter's profession," Mitch said, eyes narrowed.

"Indeed I do. More's the pity for her."

When Mitch felt her tense, his edges turned rougher and he couldn't keep his mouth shut. "If that's the way you feel, why bother with the program?"

"It wasn't my idea. Believe me." Without giving his daughter a look he said, "If it was up to me, you'd be out. And frankly this is all just a waste of time and money, in my estimation. I don't expect any results and we'll be back to square one, which is asking for your resignation."

"What if I prove you wrong?" Mitch asked, barely able to rein in his anger.

"I'm not wrong. And if my daughter would stop wasting her time and take my advice to find a real profession, one worthy of respect, she would be much better off." His mouth thinned in distaste when he looked at Sam. "Now if you'll excuse me, there's someone I need to talk to. I'll see you later, Samantha."

Mitch was about to follow and felt Sam's hand on his arm. "Don't," she whispered.

"Just one good shot," he said through clenched teeth.

"Please. No—" Her voice caught and abruptly she turned and walked in the opposite direction.

Mitch didn't realize she was leaving until she stopped at the table, grabbed her purse and wrap, then hurried toward the exit. He followed her out the double doors, down two sets of escalators, through the casino and past the registration desk. For a small woman she went pretty damn fast in her high heels. Before he knew it she was through the front doors and outside. When he caught up with her, he heard her say something to the attendant about a cab.

"Sam—"

"Go away, Mitch." She wouldn't look at him.

"I'll walk you to your car."

"It's not here. I came with him." Her voice was unsteady and she caught her top lip between her teeth. "I think…it's better if I take a cab home."

"Ignore him."

"Easy for you to say—" She had her back to him.

"Okay. It is easy for me. I'm an objective observer. In spite of the fact that you think I have the sensibility of a water buffalo, I realize that you're dealing with an emotional component. But, Sam—" He put a hand on her shoulder and gently turned her toward him.

Her eyes were moist with tears and something tightened in his chest.

He'd been susceptible to a woman's tears a time or two.

His ex-wife. His mother when she pleaded with him time and again to help Robbie. Pain sliced through him at the memory. He didn't trust tears. Female tears were tools of manipulation. Interesting the first syllable of that word was *man*. He should just walk away and let her get a cab. Let her deal with the real water buffalo in her life on her own terms. The words were on the tip of his tongue until he saw her mouth tremble and her struggle to control it.

Instead of "good night" he said, "I'm taking you home."

Chapter Four

Mitch was driving on Interstate 15 south and nearing the turnoff to the 215 Beltway before Sam said anything. The only reason she did was to give him transition directions.

"Take the Beltway east. Toward Henderson."

"Okay. Which exit?" he asked.

"Green Valley Parkway.

She'd been a blubbering idiot; there was no recovery from that. Except that after speaking she felt the lack of conversation.

"Nice car." It was a two-seater Mercedes. Red. Hot. A chick magnet.

He glanced over. "Thanks."

She glanced over at him, all sexy in the driver's seat. He'd taken off his black tie and released the first button on his pleated white shirt. Lights from the freeway danced over the angles of his handsome face and created enigmatic shadows as he aggressively guided the purring machine along the transition curve to the 215 and home.

She couldn't believe she'd let her father get under her skin like that. He was the same thoughtless man she'd learned to compensate for a long time ago. He hadn't changed, but she'd lost it, and that hadn't happened for a very long time. The only variable was Mitch. Something about being criticized in front of him had pushed her over the edge.

Yet Mitch had come to her rescue. Sir Galahad in a hot, red car. She should probably make conversation, but her emotions were still unstable and held together by a thread. The best thing she could do was gut it out until she was alone. Finally, Mitch exited the freeway.

"Turn right. It's the last apartment complex before Horizon Ridge."

He did as she directed, then slowed to a stop at the gate. She gave him the number code and the gates swung open, allowing him inside. A few more directions later and he parked in front of her unit.

"I'm sorry about—" Tears welled in her eyes and emotion thickened in her throat. One humiliating incident tonight wasn't enough? Another meltdown was pathetically close. She was two for two. It was time to give Sir Galahad the night off. "Thanks for the ride," she whispered.

That was all she could manage without losing it. She slid from the car and shut the door, then hurried to the stairway leading up to her apartment. Grabbing her long skirt in one hand so as not to trip, she quickly climbed the stairs to the second floor. Behind her she heard a car door close and footsteps following. She stopped at Unit 27 and opened her purse, then moisture blurred her vision. But Mitch was there, big and strong and smelling so good, so masculine.

Without a word, he took her bag and easily located her key. After opening the door, he reached in and flipped the light switch on, then rested his warm palm on the small of her back, guiding her inside.

She took a deep breath and met his gaze. "You've certainly gone above and beyond the call of duty tonight."

"It's the least I can do."

No, the least would have been to let her take a cab. And she wished he had. "Thank you for everything. Good night—"

"Are you throwing me out, Ms. Ryan?"

"Yes. I'd really like to be alone."

He set her purse on the sofa table in the entryway, then noticed the decanter of brandy and glasses. Without asking permission, he poured some of the liquor into two snifters and handed one to her.

"No, thanks, I—"

"Doctor's orders," he said, touching his glass to hers, before glancing around. "Nice place."

Following his gaze she took in the beige-and-maroon chenille corner group, the circular oak table and four chairs in the dining area, distressed mahogany buffet with battered copper accessories on top. She'd painted the walls a harvest gold with one wall covered in a bold burnt orange. It was colorful, warm and inviting.

"My father h-hates it," she said.

Mitch moved closer and the spark of anger in his eyes was clearly visible in the dim light. In spite of the simmering hostility, his touch was gentle when he crooked a finger beneath her glass and urged it to her lips for a sip.

"Your father is a first-class idiot."

Maybe, but he was the idiot who'd raised her and she loved him for that. She owed him a lot. "Thanks for getting the valet to let my father know not to wait for me."

His mouth pulled tight for a moment but all he said was, "You're welcome."

"And thanks for not giving me too hard a time when I insisted the valet tell him that I wasn't feeling well."

"As opposed to you'd rather walk barefoot on glass than get in the car with him?"

"Yes," she said. "I know you don't understand—"

"You're right. I don't get it. You're bright and beautiful and witty. I don't understand why you let him get away with treating you like a ditz."

"He's entitled to his opinion about what I do."

"That doesn't give him the right to be vicious."

She took another sip of brandy and felt it warm her inside. The look Mitch was giving her heated her, too, in an entirely different way.

"How is what my father did tonight different from what you do when you have a strong conviction about someone or something? I've seen you in action and there was no holding back."

"You're not doing something that gets someone hurt," he defended. "If people would just stop and think—"

"In your opinion. It's the facts as you see them and when you unload that opinion, people's feelings get hurt."

He ran his fingers through his hair, then drained his glass and set it on the coffee table she'd painted in a deep, cocoa-brown. "Trust me, my behavior is nothing like your father. He's an ass."

"I can't argue with that. And yet he's on a mission to raise money for a cancer treatment center to honor the memory of the woman he loved. So he's an ass with shades of gray."

"There's got to be something in it for him," Mitch said.

"Tonight's event was a lot of work. I hope he does get something out of it."

"You were having a good time until he showed up."

She nodded. "Yeah."

He moved in front of her, close enough to feel the warmth of his body. "If I remember right, you'd just said that I was a guy who saves lives. And that makes me a—"

"What?" she asked.

"That's what I'd like to know. You didn't get a chance to finish the thought."

Hero was what she'd meant to say. And tonight he'd shown her he was one of the good guys outside of work, too. She finished the brandy in her glass and set it beside his. The warmth lingered inside her along with the sadness.

"That's not all I didn't finish." Her eyes filled again as she remembered how happy she'd been when Mitch held her in his arms and guided her around the dance floor. He was looking puzzled, waiting for her to explain. And all she could say was, "We left our dessert—"

Her voice caught and she turned away. "Please don't think I'm ungrateful, but I'd really like to be by myself now."

"Don't, Sam—" He moved behind her, curving his fingers around her arms. "Don't cry. He isn't worth it."

When he turned her toward him, a single tear slid down her cheek. He cupped her face in his hands and brushed the moisture away with his thumb as his gaze skipped over her face. Staring at her, he shook his head as he let out a sound that was part exasperation, part groan. Then he lowered his mouth to hers.

The touch was soft, tentative, testing until her sigh of surrender. Then the contact turned into an explosion of heat and need. His arms came around her, crushing her to him and she'd never felt safer or more secure. She'd never needed like she did now. No questions. No overthinking. She'd never lost control this way, not even with the man she'd almost married. This was simple, basic lust—easy to understand and explain. And best of all when she wanted him with every fiber of her being there was no room for anything but the insatiable yearning.

He kissed her, then ran his tongue over her lips, coaxing them open. He didn't hesitate to plunge inside, giving as much as he took. She held on to the lapels of his jacket for all she was worth, enjoying the primal strength of him hidden by the sophisticated clothing. He was like a big present just waiting to be opened and the anticipation built along with a delicious pressure deep inside.

They were both breathing hard when he pulled back and studied her face. "Sam—"

"I know."

And she did. Sliding her hands over his chest, she pushed his tuxedo jacket from his shoulders, letting it drop on the carpet. He reached out and pulled the pins from her hair and she shook the strands free. Passion etched his face as he slid one finger beneath the strap of her gown and down her arm before tugging it over her breasts and hips until it pooled at her feet. Reaching behind her, he unhooked her strapless bra, allowing her breasts to spill free before his hands were there to cup and caress her.

Sam sucked in a delicious breath when he stroked an aroused nipple. Then he bent and took it into his mouth, the pleasure so intense she could hardly stand it.

She undid the buttons on his shirt with shaking fingers and he yanked it off before she rested her hands on his broad chest, the dusting of hair tickling her palms. He kissed her again and her lips parted, allowing him access. Taking full advantage, he dipped his tongue inside and stroked until liquid heat poured through her, leaving her thighs shaking and a pressure building deep inside.

She'd never needed like this before, never wanted the way she wanted Mitch.

She brushed her fingertips across his abdomen and over his waist, feeling his spasm of response as she traced the sensitive spot just above the waistband of his slacks. When she slid a finger beneath, he sucked in a breath. In a heartbeat he swept off the rest of her clothes and his, then lowered her to the carpet with her dress, his jacket and everything else around them. All she wanted was him inside her. All she could think about was relieving the pressure he'd built in the center of her being.

With his knee he parted her legs, then slid into her where she welcomed him with open arms and waiting warmth. He plunged deeper, drove her higher until her sudden and unexpectedly swift release exploded into a fireball that shattered into a thousand points of light. Before she was back in one piece he thrust once more, then stilled above her and groaned out his own satisfaction.

For several moments he simply held her tight, his body a solid sweet weight on her. Then he rested his forehead to hers and she felt more than saw his smile.

"You okay?" he asked.

"Yeah."

The response was automatic, but she realized it was the truth. He'd wanted her. He'd told her she was bright and beautiful and the words were a balm to her battered soul. She was very all right and couldn't regret what they'd just done. He kissed her nose, then took her lips in an achingly tender touch.

His slow, sexy grin was a wicked challenge. "Are you still sorry about missing dessert?"

She shook her head. "That was twice as good with none of the calories."

"Good answer. As much as I hate to, it's time to go. I have to be at the hospital before God."

When he levered himself up and reached for his clothes, she grabbed the afghan from the arm of her sofa and wrapped it around her naked shoulders. After dressing, he looked down at her, all satisfied male. "Next time I'll make sure there's a bed."

She blinked up at him. "Next time?"

"I'm a confident guy."

"There can't be a next time."

"Why not?" He reached down a hand and pulled her to her feet, staring into her eyes for a long time. "I want to see you, Sam."

The problem with losing control and rational thought was that when both returned, everything came back into focus in a rush. She couldn't regret what they'd done, but… Why did there always have to be a but?

She shook her head. "That's not smart."

"I believe it would be one of the smartest things I've done in a very long time."

"This was a huge mistake, Mitch," she said, looking at her bra and panties still on the floor. "You're a client of my firm."

"But not *your* client. It's not an ethical violation."

"But it's a gray area." She bit her lip. "So very, very gray."

"Then let's just cut to black. I want to see you. Personally. On a date. You, me, dinner. Maybe a movie. A show. I hear there's a new musical at the Venetian. I'll get tickets. We could—"

"No. Let's just chalk it up to—whatever—and move on."

He dragged his fingers through his hair. "I'm not going to argue with you."

That would be a first. "Good."

"It's late. You're tired." He threaded his fingers through her hair and cupped her face in his hands as he dropped a tender kiss on her lips. He brushed his thumbs gently over her cheeks before saying, "We'll talk about it another time. Good night, Sam. Lock the door after me."

She did, then leaned against it with a sigh. The light caught the glitter of her gown in the middle of her living room floor, evidence of how bad this idea had been. While he was kissing her she'd had no room for regrets but now she was flooded with them. He made her forget everything except being in his arms.

She'd only wanted to be with him, so desperately she hadn't given a single thought to making it into the bedroom. Not only was he a client of her firm, the intensity of the physical attraction simmering between them made her too vulnerable. Thank goodness he wasn't *her* client because she didn't have to see him again. That would be a very bad idea.

Whistling tunelessly, Mitch leaned an elbow on the counter at the nurse's station in the E.R. It was a slow day and two women were working there. A redhead, Tina, was inputting computer information and the one kneeling on the floor, straightening out a cupboard, had brown hair. She was kind of new and he thought her name was Jill. He remembered giving her a hard time after car accident victims were brought in when the trauma bay wasn't stocked the way he liked it and his orders weren't followed fast enough. He had ridden her pretty hard more than once. She hadn't looked up, but knew he was there because her shoulders were so rigid one touch would snap her in two.

He stopped whistling. "Jill?"

Her hands stilled and her body went tight. It wouldn't surprise him to see her crawl into the cupboard, but she met his gaze. "Dr. Tenney—"

"Call me Mitch." He smiled at her with all the charm he had.

Blue eyes widened as she rested her hands in her lap. "Okay. Is there something you needed, Doctor?"

"Yeah. I just want to say you did a good job this morning with that asthmatic kid."

"I did?" she asked warily.

He nodded. "By the book. You got respiratory therapy down here stat and we had everything before anyone asked for it. I just wanted to say thanks."

She looked as if he'd sucker punched her. "Y-you're welcome."

"Keep up the good work."

"Yes, Doctor."

He sighed and figured it would take a little more effort on his part before the deer-caught-in-headlights look disappeared. "Thanks for your efforts. You, too, Tina."

"Okay," they both said, exchanging a glance that clearly said "who is this alien creature?"

"Okay, then." He turned away and started whistling again as he walked down the hall to the break room.

He poured himself a cup of coffee and picked up the newspaper on the table. Flipping through it, he stopped at the Nevada section, the page showing Las Vegas social events with photos of last night's hospital function. Arnold Ryan was in three out of four with his smooth, suck-you-in, phony smile. Mitch wished Sam would tell him to go to hell. If the guy ever treated her that way again while he was around, Mitch planned to do it for her.

Sam.

He smiled as visions of her filled his head. Shining, shimmering Sam with her delicate curves and sweet smile. Oh, what a night. And he'd actually intended to make an appearance, have a drink, be sure he was seen and get the heck outta there. Then the crowd parted and he spotted Sam.

The break room door opened and Rhonda Levin walked in. She was a brown-eyed bleached blonde in her late thirties, plump, pretty and plainspoken. She didn't take any of his crap and he respected her for that. The expression on her face made him wonder what he'd done.

"Dr. Mitch—"

He put the paper down and gave her his full attention. "Hi."

"Hi, yourself."

"How are you?" he asked.

"Just dandy. You?"

"Great. Never better." He hadn't felt this good for a long time.

Rhonda put her hands on her ample hips. "What's going on, Mitch?"

"Not much. It's slow today. That's nice for a change. Gives the staff a chance to stand down and take a deep breath."

"Speaking of the staff—"

He held up a hand. "I don't want to hear it. I've been completely charming. If anyone is complaining about me they need to take a happy pill because I can't *be* any better than this. What—"

"Since when do you say please and thank you?"

"Someone's ticked because I was polite?"

Rhonda shook her head. "No. There was an unconfirmed report that you were whistling in the halls."

He frowned. "There's a rule against that?"

"No. But barking is your style. You never whistle and it's scaring my nurses."

"I didn't do anything. I swear." He grinned. "Trust me."

One corner of her mouth quirked up. "Not the words to inspire confidence, Doc."

"Seriously, all is well. I'm an easygoing guy."

"Since when?"

Since sleeping with Sam last night, he thought.

He looked at Rhonda and continued to work his innocent expression. "I've always been an easygoing guy."

"Maybe that guy is in there somewhere. But we haven't seen him since your brother died." Rhonda wasn't the type to sugarcoat it and she didn't now.

He appreciated her honesty. Mostly. But his gut twisted with the bitter memory of a death he hadn't been able to prevent, the person he'd most wanted to help and couldn't. "I've put it in the past and turned over a new leaf."

Rhonda's eyes narrowed suspiciously. "Oh?"

"Yeah. Mean Mitch is gone. Cool, calm, peaceful, placid Mitch has taken over."

"Now you're starting to scare *me*. Do you have a schizoid thing going on?"

"I'm the same lovable guy I've always been."

She sat down in the metal folding chair beside him. "Then who can we thank for the new and improved, peaceful, calm Mitch?"

Sam, he thought again.

He looked at Rhonda and knew he couldn't tell her about great sex with Samantha Sunshine. That was unprofessional and a gentleman just didn't spread stuff like that around.

"It wasn't that hard a question, Mitch. What's going on with you?"

He folded his arms over his chest. "If I wasn't serene Mitch, this interrogation could seriously tick me off. You can't satisfy some people. They complain to the powers that be if I'm abrasive and demanding. They cower behind you if I'm charming and polite. What does a guy have to do around here to get you off his back?"

"Tell me who gets the flowers to express the staff's gratitude for this change in you."

He pointed at her. "I get it. You're fishing for gossip. You want details to spice up lunch conversation."

"Maybe." Her mouth twitched. "It helps pass the time in an interesting way."

"You'll get no dirt from me," he said in his best I'm-above-all-that voice.

"Seriously? You're not going to dish about who she is?"

"What makes you think it's a she?"

"Oh, please. This is me. You got some." She stared at him and her gaze was knowing. "If not last night, recently you did the horizontal hokeypokey. If I was chirping like a happy little bird at everyone you'd be all over me for a name."

She had his number. "The fact that you're right doesn't mean I'm going to sing like a canary."

"So there is someone?"

"I'm not talking." He pressed his lips together.

"You're not denying, either." The pager at her waist let out a shrill noise and she plucked it off to check the display. "Boy, are you one lucky son of a gun." She stood up. "This isn't over, Doc."

He watched her leave the room and realized she could interrogate him until hell wouldn't have it, but no way he was talking about Sam. And there was no question she was responsible for the way he felt.

The sex was great. Better than great. Her warm, willing, sexy curvy little body snuggled in his arms was about the biggest turn-on in the universe. Being with her had pushed away the darkness that always threatened to pull him in. But he couldn't quite snuff out the thought that this metamorphosis from mean to serene Mitch had nothing to do with sex and everything to do with Sam.

He wanted more of her; he wanted to see her again. But she'd turned him down flat. So he'd go to plan B. If she wouldn't go out with him, he would find another way to spend time with her.

Chapter Five

Sam made some notes on the session with her last client, a working mom whose husband wasn't pulling his share of the domestic load. They'd talked about strategies to engage him in the day-to-day difficulties of three children, two pets, two careers and a big house. The woman had a job she loved but was considering giving it up to better meet the demands of getting kids to ballet, piano lessons, baseball and soccer practice, not to mention keeping their environment decent enough to meet basic health department standards. She was typical of the modern woman with all the stresses and frustrations.

And everything Sam had always wanted.

Her goal was to highlight the positives and joy of this life while pointing out ways in which dad/husband could help with the burden. A woman should be able to have it all just like a man.

There was a knock on her office door. She glanced at her wristwatch and realized it was nearly 7:00 p.m., after office hours. "Come in, Darlyn."

When the door opened, her boss wasn't standing there. "Hi," Mitch said.

Her heart started hammering the way it always did when he showed up. If it wasn't so exciting, it would be damned annoying. Actually, it was still damned annoying. And completely unacceptable. This was Monday, two days since she'd last seen him and, up until this moment, a good start to her work week.

"What are you doing here?" she asked.

"I just had my appointment with your boss."

"Oh."

So, he had an excuse to be on the premises. That still didn't give him a pass to invade her space. She'd told him they couldn't see each other. Difficult man. Her father was bad enough, but he was family. She'd thought he'd prepared her to handle a difficult man, but Mitch Tenney was difficult in an entirely new and completely different way. An exciting way. But he was a problem she didn't want or need. And she'd told him so. Right after he'd made love to her until she'd been putty in his hands and purred like a contented kitten.

The memory of seeing him naked started the blood pumping through her veins and brought a flush of warmth to her cheeks. He looked darn good dressed, too. The worn jeans, white cotton shirt and black leather jacket worked for her. No, not for her. It was strictly an observation. He could be any guy on the street who was public eye candy.

But she didn't sleep with just any eye candy. She'd slept with *him*. And she had a little bit of a crush/hero-worship thing going on. Somewhere in the back of her mind she'd known seeing him was inevitable. If there was any positive to him showing up now it was getting this first postcoital meeting over with. She'd had no time to anticipate and fret about whether or not her hair and makeup were perfect. Oh, for Pete's sake. It so didn't matter what she looked like. She was a professional, not a hormonal teenager.

"How are you, Sam?"

Acting like a hormonal teenager, thank you very much. "Fine. And you?"

"Good."

"How was your weekend?" he asked.

"Fine. And yours?" Automatic words that she desperately wanted back when a satisfied grin turned up the corners of his mouth.

"Great. I had to work Sunday, but Saturday night was very nice."

Yeah. For her, too. She had to get this back on a professional footing. "And how was work?"

"Quiet. But I was in a great mood. All the nurses are talking about it."

As if she needed another reason to blush. Show some spine, Sam, she ordered. Sitting up straight, she folded her hands and set them on the desk. "You should attend fund-raisers more often, Mitch. That philanthropic spirit feeds the soul and shines through."

"I'll keep that in mind."

"Good," she said, nodding. They stared at each other for several moments and for the life of her all she could think about was how sexy he looked with his shoulder braced against the doorjamb.

"Aren't you going to ask me about my session with Darlyn?"

Duh. "Sorry. Of course. How did it go?"

"Okay."

"Wow. Praise like that will do wonders for her professional reputation. Corporations all over Las Vegas will be clamoring for her services."

"Someone took a sassy pill," he observed, one dark eyebrow raised.

"Not yet, but I could be persuaded."

"It's good to hear you're in a mood to be won over." He moved then, into her office and around the desk.

"What are you doing?"

"Making lifestyle changes as ordered."

He pulled her to her feet, then took her hand and tugged her down the hall to Darlyn's office. He knocked on the door and when the word came to enter, he pulled her inside along with him.

Darlyn looked up from the paperwork on her desk. "Mitch. I thought you'd left. Was there something else you wanted to discuss?"

"Yes." Still gripping her hand, he urged Sam forward. "I want to request that Sam be my counselor."

"I see." In her late forties, Darlyn Marshall looked at least ten years younger. Her auburn hair was short and no-nonsense, like the woman herself, but her warm, cinnamon-colored eyes kept her from looking too severe. "Do you mind if I ask why you're making the request?"

"It has to be said that wasn't my idea." Sam pulled her hand from Mitch's. "I didn't know he was going to do this, Darlyn. Obviously you're the best—"

"It's okay, Sam. There's no ego involved. I'm simply curious." Darlyn looked at Mitch. "So, Doctor, would you care to explain your reasoning?"

"I'm glad you asked." He slid his fingers into the pockets of his jeans. "Let me say up front that it's not a conflict with you in any way. I feel that my progress would be faster and the counseling more effective if I worked with Sam. It's as simple as that."

"I see." Darlyn tapped her pen on the pad in front of her. "Sam? What do you think?"

"You're the best. Let's leave well enough alone," she answered.

Mitch shook his head. "I disagree. Correct me if I'm wrong. This is your sphere of expertise after all, but doesn't a person need to feel completely comfortable in a situation to have a successful outcome?"

"That's true," Darlyn confirmed. "And we do our best at Marshall Management to match client and counselor. But I believe I'm the most qualified to assist you in making the changes necessary to enhance your professional life."

"I see." Mitch nodded thoughtfully. "Then I'm in the awkward position of having to make a choice about whether or not to continue with Marshall or take my business to a competitor."

Sam nearly gave herself whiplash as she turned to glare at him. He could go outside the hospital contract if he wanted. Who was going to stop him? Harsh words hovered on the tip of her tongue, but she was professional enough to hold back. Being a consummate professional, Darlyn showed no reaction to his ultimatum.

After several moments of silence, she said, "Sam, may I speak with you alone?"

"Of course." She looked at Mitch. "Do you mind?"

"Not at all." He nodded. "Ladies."

When he'd left and closed the door behind him, Sam sat in the chair in front of her boss's desk. "I'm so sorry, Darlyn. Please don't think I'm trying to sabotage you or steal a client."

"That never occurred to me." Darlyn held up a hand. "If you were, you'd never have told me he wanted to retain your services after that very first session. When I was ill."

"I thought you should know."

"Full disclosure."

"Yes. Trust is paramount in any relationship—personal or professional." Sam linked her fingers in her lap. "The thing is, he's a difficult individual. I believe he wants me because he feels that I'll be more easily handled."

And based on how little effort it took to get her into bed he'd be right about that. Even cutting herself some slack that he'd caught her at an emotional low point, and technically she'd violated no ethical code of conduct by sleeping with him, she wasn't prepared to reveal to her boss what had happened. She simply wanted Darlyn to pull rank and make the decision to continue working with Mitch. Call his bluff.

"I hear what you're saying," Darlyn said. "You certainly know yourself, but I don't necessarily agree that you're a pushover for Dr. Tenney." The words should have been reassuring. "The thing is, Sam, my goal in going out on my own was to grow the business. Getting the hospital contract was a very big step in doing that."

"I see."

"Having an unsuccessful outcome with our very first challenging client will not earn capital in terms of establishing confidence or a positive reputation in this town."

Sam took no satisfaction from the fact that she'd said almost the same thing to Mitch just a short time ago. She had a bad feeling about this. "And?"

"He has the right to request whomever he wants to work with. I'd consider it a personal favor if you would agree to his terms."

Her heart dropped. "You know I'd do anything you asked."

"I know." Darlyn smiled. "And I know this man pushes some professional buttons for you."

Some personal ones, too. But she wouldn't say so. "Yeah. He does," she agreed.

"If there was any other way, I wouldn't ask you to do it."

"I know." There was no point in trying to wiggle out of this. Her back was against the wall. "I'll do my best."

"That's a given. Thanks, Sam."

"Don't mention it."

She stood and walked back to her office. It shouldn't surprise her that Mitch was still there, but his presence took her aback.

"So, what's the verdict?" he asked.

"As if you didn't already know."

"I take it you're my new counselor?"

"Oh, please."

"Excellent," he said with a grin. "So I guess we'll be seeing a lot of each other."

"Not the way you mean." She looked up at him and got a smidgen of satisfaction when the grin disappeared and his eyes narrowed. The fact that he'd completely disregarded her ultimatum—wishes, needs, whatever you want to call it—was proof that this was wrong. The only way to make it right was to lose herself in the job.

"You can make an appointment on your way out," she said.

If there was any good news, it was that he'd changed the professional dynamic and there was no way she would sleep with him again. No matter how he tempted her personally, she'd never jeopardize her career. Showing her father that she wasn't a flake took top priority. Violating the ethics of her office wouldn't get the job done.

Mitch Tenney with his devil grin and killer bod might tempt her to compromise something she'd worked so long and hard for but she'd never give in to it.

Mitch wanted more of Sam, but not here at the hospital. He leaned against the wall outside of trauma bay three and studied her, taking notes on him. She'd told him that before his next appointment she needed to observe him at work—or as he liked to say to her, in his natural habitat.

She looked so darn cute with her square, black-framed glasses on her turned up nose and curls pulled back in a ponytail that skimmed the spot on her neck that he knew was particularly sensitive. If the E.R. wasn't teeming with employees, he'd take that spot out for another spin and see if history would repeat itself and he could coax a moan from her Cupid's bow mouth.

He'd really enjoy giving her something else to do with her hands instead of writing down everything he said and did, evaluating his people skills she called it. Have clipboard will document every interaction. When he'd insisted on her as his counselor, he'd figured to spend time with her and dispel whatever reservations she had about seeing him. But being shadowed on the job wasn't exactly what he'd had in mind.

"How's the hand?" he asked.

She glanced at him and pushed her glasses up on her nose. "What?"

"Got writer's cramp yet?" he said, pointing to the clipboard. "You're taking a lot of notes. I can't imagine that someone with the flu, or a broken arm and a bump on the head, is grist for the great American novel."

She held the clipboard to her breasts like armor. "It's not fiction. In fact the material I'm gathering on you will be incredibly helpful in your retraining."

"Retraining?" He folded his arms over his chest. "What am I? A seal?"

"You're a talented and dedicated emergency room doctor whose people skills need tweaking."

"You think I'm talented?" he asked.

"No one disputes that," she said, a faint pink creeping into her cheeks.

She was remembering that night, too, and he was glad not to be the only one. He sincerely hoped the *talented* she was referring to was about what they'd done horizontally. "And dedicated?"

"Mostly I think you need some pointers in how to get along well with others."

"I see. So—"

"Dr. Mitch." Rhonda walked up to them and looked Sam over. "Hello, again."

"Hi." Sam smiled in her usual friendly way, giving no indication she was aware of the grilling she was about to get.

Mitch had been dreading this encounter because his nurse didn't miss anything. "Did you need me for something, Rhonda?"

"No." She tucked a strand of bleached blond hair behind her ear and turned her attention to Sam. "I remember you from a couple of weeks ago. Samantha?"

"Right. It's nice to see you again. And call me Sam."

"The pleasure is all mine, Sam, if you're the one responsible for the positive change in our Mitch."

He barely managed to keep in the groan. "I'm the same lovable guy."

"He's made some improvement?" Sam asked, ignoring him.

"Improvement?" Rhonda scoffed. "It's a miracle. He dispenses praise and encouragement like he's being paid per compliment."

Sam jotted something down on her clipboard, then looked up and smiled. "I'm so glad."

"And just the other day he was actually whistling." Rhonda slid him a wicked look just to let him know she suspected that Sam was the woman he'd been unwilling to name. "Mitch is so not a whistler that the event was memorable."

"I can't tell you how happy it makes me to hear that," Sam said, smiling brightly.

"Yeah. He's like the bluebird of happiness these days." Rhonda reached for the pager at her waist and glanced at the display. "Paramedics are on the way. ETA two minutes. I'll page you when we've got the patient ready for you. Gotta go. Good to see you again, Sam."

"Same here." As the nurse hurried down the hall, Sam looked up at him and smiled. "See. A little tweaking goes a long way."

There was tweaking and there was tweaking, he thought. "Look, Sam, my shift is over in about thirty minutes. Have dinner with me."

"No." She walked away and he caught up with her in front of the double doors that separated patient trauma rooms from the waiting area.

He put a hand on her shoulder and she slowly turned. "No? Just like that? Not even an explanation?"

"I'm your relationship coach."

"Exactly. You should know better than to be so abrupt. A polite 'I'm sorry I can't because I have other plans' would be far less hurtful."

"It would also be a lie. I don't have plans tonight."

"Then have dinner with me." He folded his arms over his chest as he looked down and met her amused gaze. "You have to eat."

"I definitely do. But not with you."

"You'd rather eat alone?" he asked.

She started to say something, then shook her head. "That question is like asking someone if they stopped beating their wife. But I'm going to answer honestly. No, I don't especially enjoy eating by myself." She held up a hand when he opened his mouth to seize the opportunity. "But we have a professional relationship and I won't cross the line into personal with you. So don't go there, Dr. Mitch."

"Who says it's personal? We'd simply be two people sharing a meal." He snapped his fingers. "We could even make it a working dinner. You could tweak me while we're at it. Critique my table manners."

The corners of her mouth twitched, clearly indicating she was having a lot of difficulty holding back a smile. "Has anyone ever mentioned that you're incorrigible?"

"My ex-wife," he said.

"You were married?"

"Yeah." Not smart to bring that up when he was trying to plead his case for dinner. He might be a son of a bitch, but Barbara had done something unforgivable. "And before you assume it went south because of me, let me say that I'll take part of the responsibility for the problems, but she made the relationship unsalvageable."

"Okay." She met his gaze. "Has anyone else said you're incorrigible?"

The double doors whispered open and someone walked through. "Mitch?"

The familiar female voice got his attention and he turned. "Mom."

Las Vegas Metro Detective Ellen Tenney was almost as tall as him. She was in her late fifties with short brown hair that she wore in a no-nonsense style, fitting her job and temperament, along with her navy suit and low-heeled black shoes. Blue eyes so like his own looked back at him, filled with disappointment, anger and reproach. At least that's what he saw.

He felt Sam's eyes on him and knew he didn't have a snowball's chance in hell of avoiding an introduction. "Detective Ellen Tenney, this is Samantha Ryan. Sam, this is my mother."

Giving no indication she'd noticed his omission of who she really was, Sam held out her hand. "It's nice to meet you, Detective Tenney."

"Likewise," Ellen said.

"I'm working with Mitch," Sam explained.

"A nurse?"

"No." Hesitating, she slid him a quick look, then said, "It's a program through the hospital that we're teaming up on."

"I see." Her expression said she had more questions. That's what a detective did, but she didn't ask.

"What are you doing here, Mom?"

"An assault victim was just brought in. I'm here to interview her. Take the statement."

"Get in line. I'll have to examine her first."

"Okay."

There was an awkward silence. He recalled his first time in Sam's office and deliberately not talking to rattle her. The older woman with the cool, blue-eyed stare had taught him the technique. Since Robbie died, the look had turned icy, and awkward silence was their primary mode of communication. He glanced at Sam and thought this was a hell of a time for her to be here taking notes.

Since he was getting critiqued, he might as well make an effort. "How've you been, Mom?"

"Fine."

He waited, but there was no reciprocation. Ellen Tenney could benefit from spending a little time with a relationship coach.

"I guess things are busy at the cop shop?"

She nodded. "Here, too, looks like."

"Some."

Sam glanced between them. "Mercy Medical is lucky to have your son working here, Detective."

"Oh?" Even Sam's sunshine couldn't thaw his mother. But that was about him.

"Yes. The first day I met him he saved the life of a little boy."

"It's good you could help," Ellen said.

Even though he couldn't save hers, Mitch thought. He knew he was a good doctor, but not good enough to get his twin brother to give up drugs. His mother had begged him time and again to help Robbie. Mitch was the responsible one. He was the smart one. It was his fault that over and over Robbie had slipped up and gone back to using. And that last time he paid the ultimate price.

Before he could comment, the pager at his waist vibrated and he looked at the display. "They need me in the trauma bay."

"Okay," Ellen said. "Let me know when I can talk to your patient."

He nodded. "'Bye, Mom."

"Nice to meet you, Detective," Sam said, hurrying after him.

Not even Sam's sunshine could break through the funk that settled over him. He worked his ass off to cheat death every time he walked through the door of a patient's room. He was successful a lot of the time but losing his brother would haunt him for the rest of his life. Ellen blamed him, but the bitch of it was that Mitch blamed himself more than she ever could. Death beat him. He'd failed.

Glancing down, he looked at Sam and felt himself slipping off the hero pedestal he hadn't even realized he was on. Suddenly it was very important that she never find out how badly he'd failed.

Chapter Six

Sam looked at the clock on her office wall between the "Success is the Intelligent Use of Mistakes" and the "Obstacles are Those Frightful Things You See When You Take Your Eyes Off Your Goals" posters. She was so a "do as I say not as I do" person. Her goal was to be successful, but agreeing to work with Mitch had put a major obstacle in her path.

Why in the world was he pursuing her so persistently? He'd already gotten her into bed—so to speak. If he was after Round Two, the man who wouldn't take no for an answer was doomed to disappointment. He'd pushed and she was his counselor. She wouldn't cross the ethical line into his bed, but it wouldn't be easy to resist.

And resist she must because he was her next appointment and due here any minute. Now he spent a good portion of their sessions trying to convince her they should go out. At least he'd done that the other day at the hospital, until his mother had shown up. Then things got really tense and awkward. What was that about? He'd actually looked relieved when the page came to see a patient.

"Hi." And there he was in the doorway.

Looking at him was the only uncomplicated part of this relationship. He was gorgeous, plain and simple. The wind had blown his dark, wavy hair into sexy disarray and his navy T-shirt outlined the contours of his broad chest and highlighted the impressive muscles in his biceps. His jeans were a combination of light blue and white where the denim was worn in the most interesting places. And whether she saw him in a tux, scrubs, jeans and a T-shirt, or nothing at all, just seeing him made her yearn to be in his arms. The realization hit her deep and hard. *That* was the really complicated part.

He lifted a hand. "I have an appointment to see you."

"I know." She pulled her thoughts back from the danger zone and reminded herself to keep her eyes on the goal. Smiling, she said, "Hi."

"Can I come in?"

"Of course." She held out a hand, indicating the chairs in front of her desk. "Have a seat."

Without a word, he walked in and chose the chair on the left. She only noticed because nine out of ten people would have gone to the right. Not Mitch.

"How's everything, Sunshine?"

Just like that she was a conflict counselor in conflict. She wanted to ask him not to call her that because it started off the session on a personal note. On the other hand she didn't want to make it an issue. Mitch was sharp and not much got by him. If he sensed any weakness, he'd use it against her and take control. Eyes on the goal.

"Everything is great," she said. "How about you? Things going well at work?"

"That's what I'm here to find out." He linked his fingers and rested them on his flat abdomen. "Did you read any of those notes you took?"

"Of course." She put her glasses on. "Would you like to hear them?"

"Do I have a choice?"

"Yes. But before you say no, just remember that recognizing the existing negative behavior is the first step toward changing it."

"Okay. Take your best shot." He slouched a little lower in the chair.

"I have only good things to say about how you handled the situation with the asthmatic child and the overexcited mother. You assessed the health concerns of the little girl and at the same time kept your cool and calmed the parent. It would have been understandable if you'd been sharp with her since she was clearly aggravating the situation and making the child more anxious, thereby worsening her difficulty breathing."

"That's in your notes?" he asked, looking surprised.

"It is. In essence you kept your eyes on the goal, which was taking care of your patient's needs, and refused to let the caregiver become an obstacle."

"Okay. Anything else?"

She glanced at the notes. "Yes. The construction worker who was knocked off a roof and broke his arm. You were diplomatic, sympathetic and somehow managed to bond with him over hammers and screwdrivers."

"Guys, tools." He shrugged. "No big deal."

"It is a big deal because you were able to rein in your runaway sarcasm and not compare him to Larry, Moe, or Curly."

He grinned. "How did you know I was thinking about the Three Stooges?"

"Just a guess." She wanted badly to return that smile, but held back with an effort. "The point is you didn't act on the impulse."

"I'm glad you noticed. Believe me, it wasn't easy."

"I'm sure it wasn't. And the man with the hives who was confrontational with you about the length of time he spent in the E.R...."

Sam remembered the overweight, balding, condescending man getting in Mitch's face after he'd been evaluated and received medication. He'd been kept there for observation and complained about how long it had been since anyone looked in on him. He'd been rude and mean and even she'd wanted to tell him to suck it up.

"That could have gone very badly if you hadn't validated his complaint. After that you calmly explained that in a busy emergency room patients are triaged and everyone's needs are met, with the most serious, life-threatening cases handled first. It was textbook customer service and defused the situation."

"Well, I don't know what to say."

"That's a first," she said wryly. "Frankly, I have mostly good comments."

One dark eyebrow rose. "I thought this was all about rubbing my nose in whatever I did wrong."

"Critiquing is as much about pointing out the positive as the need to improve in certain areas." She met his gaze. "You were successful in not being dictatorial, defiant or silently superior. Your manner was all about quiet strength and compassionate support."

"You said *mostly* good comments, which means some are not so good. How did I screw up?"

"It's not so much a how as a when. At a certain point there was a change in your attitude."

He sat up straighter. "You want to explain that?"

"You were different after you spoke with your mother."

"Is that in the notes?"

"Yes, although it's not something I'm likely to forget." She slid her glasses off and met his gaze. "Clearly you followed in her footsteps in a service-oriented career."

"I suppose. But I'm not sure what that has to do with anything."

"Our lives are like a puzzle and all the pieces fit together to form a whole picture."

"That sounds very Zen-like." One corner of his mouth turned up. "Is this where you tell me not to test the depth of the water with both feet?"

"This is where I ask what's going on between the two of you."

"And it's where I answer that it's off-limits." His mouth pulled into a rebellious, stubborn, straight line.

"I have to point out that the subject is fair game because every aspect of your life affects work performance."

"What affects your performance, Sam?"

She suspected he was thinking about the night her father had made her lose it. The night they'd made love. He was trying to take the heat off himself by distracting her, rattling her in a personal way. It did shake her up, but she wouldn't let him win.

"We're talking about you," she said calmly. "My job isn't in jeopardy."

Yet, she thought. And she intended to keep it that way.

He looked at her and let the silence drag out between them. She was getting used to the tactic and didn't feel the need to chatter away to fill the void. Waiting him out was getting easier.

He took her measure and must have sensed her resolve because he blew out a long breath. "How about a quid pro quo?"

"Meaning?"

"You share something, then I will."

"A professional isn't supposed to use examples from their own life," she explained.

She studied the dark intensity on his face and wavered. Whatever was causing the friction between him and his mother was at the heart of his relationship issues. She wished she could claim brilliance for the insight, but she'd been a witness to the change in him. One minute he was sweetness and light, the next he was a jerk with a capital *J*. If sharing something with him could facilitate a breakthrough…

"Okay," she said. "I'll throw you a bone."

"I'm all ears."

"School was very difficult for me and my grades were pretty much in the dumper. I thought I was stupid and slow. All the other kids could get whatever material was presented, but I couldn't."

"I think you're one of the quickest, brightest women I've ever met."

His words started a glow that warmed her from the inside out. "I'm not fishing for compliments. It's just the way it was."

"Don't tell me. Let me guess. Your stepfather reinforced the perception?"

"You're pretty quick yourself." She leaned back in her chair. "He compared me to his smart, gifted, high-achieving biological children and couldn't understand why I had so much trouble learning unless my IQ was in the slow range."

The muscle in his jaw jerked. "Yet, here you are—a relationship counselor with impeccable credentials. That isn't the performance of a woman with IQ challenges. What gives?"

"I'm dyslexic."

"That doesn't make you stupid," he pointed out.

"You're right. In high school a caring teacher recognized what was going on with me and that changed everything. I learned coping mechanisms and techniques to facilitate reading. It didn't take long after that to perform at my grade level and I was able to get into college. Studies have shown that many highly visible, incredibly successful people are dyslexic. They tap into skills other than visual and use them to thrive. Recognizing the problem was the key to success."

"And your stepfather? What did he say about it?"

Identifying the problem convinced him she would never flourish on her own. She intended to prove him wrong.

No way she was sharing that with Mitch. "Now it's your turn to talk about family. What's up with you?"

"I suppose you're not going to let me sidetrack you on this?"

"Not even for money," she agreed.

"Okay. I'll throw *you* a bone." He rested his elbows on his knees and linked his fingers. "I had a twin brother."

He was a twin? There were two Mitchs? Then she realized he said *had*. "What happened?"

"He died."

The darkness she'd seen in him before was nothing compared to what was there now. His haunted expression tugged at her heart.

"How?" she asked softly.

"It doesn't matter." He met her gaze. "You have dyslexia. My brother Robbie is dead. Quid pro quo."

And the free-exchange-of-information door slammed shut, which was not what she'd hoped for. It wasn't her job to find out his secrets and make him feel better. Her responsibility was to teach him coping skills so that when the past intruded he wouldn't take out his attitude on everyone around him.

Somehow that just wasn't good enough. Somehow she was going to find out what he was holding inside. That goal was important to her, so much more than it should be, which put the association on a personal level.

It was only a matter of time until this happened. It was why taking him on as a client had been a mistake.

* * *

Mitch's mood at work had been a lot better when Sam shadowed him. This morning had been busy and difficult. He'd seen patients with the flu who'd waited too long to seek medical intervention, and a car accident fatality with street racing involved. The most frustrating case was the toddler with suspicious injuries. He could hear Sam's voice in his head telling him not to be dictatorial, defiant, or silently superior. She'd left out tactful, but he'd reached down deep to pull out all the prudence and caution he could. Seeing that little boy's bruises had nearly pushed him over the edge but he'd channeled his rage into personally calling LV Metro and child services in that order.

He rounded the corner from the E.R. on his way to the doctor's dining room and saw Sam, and his spirits did a one-eighty. Her smile lifted the cone of darkness around him to let in the light. Then he noticed the tall, good-looking guy beside her, who had made her laugh. The one in the expensive charcoal suit and red power tie. The one with dark hair, blue eyes and a confident, cocky walk. That put a crimp in his mood. In fact when the guy put his hand at the small of her back to guide her into the cafeteria, Mitch felt a punch of jealousy that rocked him hard.

Who was this guy? The ex-fiancé? Was she going to apologize like Daddy wanted and patch things up with the serial cheater?

He should keep on walking and avoid her like bubonic plague, but suddenly he turned left instead of right and followed them. When Sam did a double take and recognized him, her smile faltered and her shoulders tensed.

"Mitch." The pulse in her throat started to flutter wildly and his spirits went up a notch.

"Hi, Sam." He eyed the guy. "Who's your friend?"

"This is my big brother. Connor Ryan." She glanced between them. "Connor, this is Mitch Tenney."

Connor held out his hand, but there was a measuring look in his eyes. "Nice to meet you."

They shook hands and Mitch returned the greeting as her big brother sized him up. Like any good, protective big brother would do. Actually this would be her stepbrother and Mitch didn't miss the irony of Ryan doing justice to sibling responsibility while Mitch had failed his identical twin miserably.

"So, Connor, I haven't seen you around here before. Do you take after your father in the hospital business?"

"No. I'm an attorney."

"Connor is with Upshaw, Marrone, Ryan and Ryan."

"I've heard of the firm," Mitch said. They were a prominent, high-profile group who handled some of the biggest corporate deals in Las Vegas, the most recent a major upscale development on the South Strip.

"And I've heard of you." Connor slid his hands into the pockets of his slacks. "You're the loose cannon of the E.R. Dad told me about."

"Guilty," Mitch said.

"He's working on that," Sam pointed out. "People can be difficult and Mitch is sometimes a little too honest."

"I just call 'em as I see 'em," he explained.

Something shifted in Connor's gaze, as he nodded. "That's not necessarily a bad thing."

Sam glanced at her watch. "I thought you had an appointment, Con. We better get something to eat before you have to go. It was nice to see you, Mitch."

Connor stopped suddenly as she was tugging him away. "Why don't you join us, Mitch?"

"I'm sure Mitch is too busy," Sam said.

"No, I'm not."

"Surely you'd rather go in the doctors' dining room where the food and service are far superior to what the peasants get here in the cafeteria," she said.

"I can suck it up," Mitch said. "If the company and conversation are worth slumming for."

"I can tell you from firsthand experience that Connor is not worth it." The words were teasing but the spirit of it wasn't reflected in her eyes.

"I'll take my chances." Mitch folded his arms over his chest and met her gaze. If she hadn't been so clearly trying to discourage him from staying, he might have let her off the hook. But something about Samantha Sunshine made him want to mess with her. "Unless there's some reason you'd rather I didn't eat with you."

Connor looked from one to the other. "Is there something going on that I should know about?"

"Absolutely not." She smiled but it was strained around the edges. "Of course you're welcome to sit with us."

"Good." Mitch straightened his halo and followed them.

After going through the food line past the steam table, grabbing drinks and paying the cashier, they sat at a table in a corner. The lunch crowd had dissipated and the cafeteria was quiet.

Connor looked at him. "So, Mitch, how are things in the E.R. business?"

"Busy." He took a bite out of his burger. "What brings the two of you here? I see Sam from time to time, but, Connor, it seems you're a long way from your legal stomping grounds."

"Dad called Sam and me over for a meeting."

"He wanted to discuss the Catherine Mary Ryan Cancer Center. Con was here for legal input and I shared personal thoughts on the project," she explained.

Con settled his paper napkin in his lap. "My sister and I decided this would be a good chance to catch up after he got through with us."

"Do you always come running when your father snaps his fingers?" Mitch asked, feeling his halo wobble. For some reason any mention of Arnold Ryan brought out the worst in him.

Connor thought for half a second, then nodded. "Pretty much. My father isn't the kind of man who's easily put off."

Mitch recalled Sam telling him about her learning disability and the less than sensitive way her stepfather handled it. Anger churned through him. "Growing up with him as a father must have been difficult."

"It had its moments," Connor agreed. "My stepmother smoothed out his rough edges. She was a warm and caring woman. The whole family felt her loss when she died."

Sam stared at the salad she was pushing around her plate. "Dad buried himself in work and channeled his energy into running Mercy Medical Center."

Connor forked up some green beans and chewed thoughtfully. "Actually, he wasn't working here then."

Sam looked at him. "Sure he was."

"No. He was working for a competitor at the time. After your mom passed away he applied for the position here at the hospital. At the same time he began proceedings to adopt you legally."

"I remember when my mother was very sick he promised her that she wouldn't have to worry about what would happen to me," Sam said. "Didn't he start the legal process before she died?"

Connor shook his head. "It's not surprising your memories

are fuzzy. You were only five or six. But I was almost sixteen and just about to get my driver's license. It's funny how a momentous event like that crystallizes memories of things that were going on at the time."

"What was going on?" she asked.

"I was learning to drive and looking for every opportunity to get behind the wheel. Dad let me chauffeur him to a meeting with an acquaintance who was on the hospital board of directors. He told Dad that image was important and he needed to stand out from the competition. Right after that I remember home evaluations by social services and court proceedings to finalize the adoption."

Mitch happened to be watching Sam's face while her brother was talking and saw the downward slide from surprise to comprehension to hurt.

"Where else did you drive him?" Mitch asked.

"Nowhere." Connor grinned. "Once I had my license I shunned the transportation gig and turned my attention to being a chick magnet with a cool car."

"Oh, right," Sam said, pushing aside her shock. "That beat-up old thing?"

"Aside from the fact that Dad wouldn't buy me wheels and it was all I could afford, that Chrysler was a classic."

"One that was always breaking down," she teased.

"*That* you remember." Connor sighed.

"Like you said, memories are crystallized by whatever events are going on. My mother had died recently and you were supposed to pick me up from first grade and never showed. I was pretty scared."

"It wasn't my fault," Connor protested.

"I know." Sam toyed with her salad some more. Not much of it had been consumed. "But that clunker was not why the girls chased you on an annoyingly regular basis."

Connor put his fork down and grinned. "I think buried somewhere in there is a compliment."

"At the risk of inflating your already inflated ego," Sam said, "you are, in fact, a hottie."

"Is that on the record?" her brother asked.

"Don't push your luck."

Though she was doing a good job of hiding her feelings, Mitch saw the shadows in her eyes. But if she wanted to discuss what was bothering her, she'd have brought it up. He'd take that as a cue that she didn't want to talk about it.

Finally, Connor looked at the expensive Rolex on his wrist. "As pleasant as it is having my ego inflated, I've got an appointment and traffic on the Fifteen freeway is a bitch this time of day." He looked at her. "Gotta run, sis."

"Coward. I was getting the best of you," she said.

"No way." He stood, then bent and kissed her cheek. "Be good. Nice to meet you, Mitch."

"Same here."

Connor hurried out and they were alone. Mitch waited as long as he could, then finally asked, "You didn't know why your stepfather adopted you, did you?"

"No." The expression in her eyes was as tender as a fresh bruise. "In spite of his impatience with me I guess I always hoped that deep down there was some affection. I never suspected that adopting me was nothing more than a bullet point on my résumé."

"Sam—" Mitch ran his fingers through his hair. What could he say? There was no way to refute the truth.

"I should have known." She pushed her uneaten salad away.

"Where in the rule book does it say that? You were a little kid. How could you possibly understand what was going on?"

"Not so much then as later," she said, meeting his gaze.

"My father never missed an opportunity to imply that I probably took after my biological father, who had no use for me. But he, Arnold Ryan, was a hero for taking me in, putting a roof over my head and making it legal."

"I'm sure he cares about you." He wasn't sure of any such thing, but didn't know what else to say.

"He cared about my mother. I'm sure about that. But the truth is pretty evident to me now."

"And that is?"

Her eyes were bleak. "He never wanted to be responsible for me at all. Ever."

Son of a bitch, he thought. The man was a coldhearted jerk. He'd get points for not abandoning Sam into the child welfare system, but that was about all. And who's to say Ryan *wouldn't* have done that if the job he'd coveted wasn't on the line? Sam had come along with the "for better or worse" vows. But when the worst happened, he'd used a sad little girl who'd just lost her mother. He agreed that Ryan would have adopted her sooner if he'd really wanted the responsibility. But he hadn't wanted it.

Any more than Mitch had wanted to be responsible for his brother.

The thought crept in and squeezed his chest.

He tried to tell himself that he wasn't a son of a bitch like Arnold Ryan. The situation with his brother had been different. Robbie was a drug addict who couldn't get the monkey off his back and Mitch had made token attempts to help but all of it failed.

Maybe there was a good reason for that. Maybe he'd never wanted to be his brother's keeper in the first place.

He was just like Sam's stepfather.

If she had any sense, she would despise him as much as he despised himself.

Chapter Seven

With a quick, irritated flourish of his hand, Mitch scratched notes in a patient's chart. "It's Halloween, Sam. Surely there's something important you have to do."

"There is. And I'm doing it right now."

"Can't you give it a rest?"

"No."

Leaning an elbow on the high counter at the nurse's station, he glanced at her. "Why?"

She straightened the black pointy hat on her head. It went with the gnarled, warty fake nose, green face paint and black cape. She'd been told that the hospital employees got into the spirit of Halloween and dressed up, jobs permitting. Her job permitted, but today hadn't been easy. There'd been a subtle shift in Mitch, as if he weren't even trying, as if he'd already fallen short of the mark.

"It's important to observe your progress at intervals during the coaching process so we can make any necessary adjustments."

He tapped his pen on the chart and met her gaze. "Is that the politically correct way of saying that I'm not making any progress?"

"Absolutely not." She shook her head and felt her hat tilt.

"Because I have. Made progress," he added. "For instance,

I could have called you a witch." He was doing his best fake innocent act, but the devilish gleam in his eyes gave him away.

"And today that would be true in every sense of the word because I'm getting into the spirit of the day." She pressed her clipboard against her chest. "At the same time I'm giving off a vibe of approachability."

"All outward evidence to the contrary." He tapped her fake nose. "Nice look, by the way. Typecasting?"

"Sticks and stones may break my bones but saying mean stuff will not discourage me from doing my job." She glanced at her notes. "Now that there's a break in the E.R. action, can we talk about what happened with that earlier patient?"

"You should have dressed up as a pit bull."

"Tsk, tsk," she said, wagging her finger. "I've got you now, my pretty."

"Not yet. But, I could easily be had." He raised his eyebrows suggestively.

"Focus, Doctor. You remember the little boy who fell and cut his knee?"

"Yeah." He blew out a long breath. "Every news station does a segment on safe Halloween costumes. How is it possible to miss the fact that kids need to be able to see where they're going when they're dressed up?"

"It's not like that mother pushed him down. She felt horribly guilty about what happened."

"She should."

"She cares about her child."

"If that were true, she'd have paid attention to the warnings and just said no to the full-face rubber werewolf mask that severely restricted his vision."

"Instead of glaring at her, perhaps it might have been more

helpful to suggest face paint for next year instead of an over-the-head mask."

"In terms of instant gratification, I find glaring much more personally satisfying."

She moved closer to him when two orderlies wheeled a bed past her. "The District in Green Valley Ranch has a party going on this afternoon and all the merchants are giving away a lot of candy. Pointing out an activity like that would be more helpful than reducing her to tears with a look."

Mitch's eyes sparked with something that made her insides quiver. "Bet my glare against your fake nose that she'll take better care of the kid next year."

"I'm sure she will, but there are ways to get the message out without making her feel like the worst mother on the planet."

"That was a tad shrill, Miss Ryan." He looked around at E.R. personnel who were glancing in their direction, then wagged a finger at her. "And right in public, too. Isn't there a rule about finding a more private place where you can rake me over the coals?"

Sam knew the gleam in his eyes meant that privacy plus Mitch Tenney equaled trouble.

But he was also right. One of the first things she'd said to him after her first observation right here in the E.R. was that he could have talked to the teenager behind closed doors.

"I'm not raking you over the coals," she said. "And thank you for reminding me that a public venue is an unacceptable location for this discussion."

"Not unacceptable for me. Just my way of letting you know I'm paying attention and making progress."

His way of toying with her, and darned if she wasn't liking every minute of it. "For the sake of discretion, let's go into the break room."

He shook his head. "That's the hard drive of the hospital rumor mill. I'll buy you a cup of cafeteria coffee."

"Make it an herbal tea and you've got yourself a deal."

"Samantha the twenty-something witch, politically correct, environmentally aware and herbally responsible. Do you have any idea how sexy that is to me?"

"Oh, please." She was onto this technique.

As long as he kept it light, she could resist. And he *was* teasing, but the word *responsible* made her think about that day he'd met her brother. When she'd found out she'd only been legally adopted because her father didn't want to look bad.

That had hurt. For years she'd made excuses for Arnold Ryan's treating her differently from his biological children. She'd believed she wasn't smart enough, or pretty enough, or good enough, when the real reason was that she wasn't his and he'd never truly wanted her to be. That was hard to hear, but she gave him credit for taking her in. It counted for something in her book.

Mitch had been incredibly sweet and supportive, right up until she'd said out loud that her father had never wanted to be responsible for her. A multitude of emotions had crossed his face. Pain. Guilt. Disgust. Instinctively she knew that all of it was directed at himself. So far all he'd told her was that he'd had a brother, a twin. And there was animosity between him and his mother. He had a couple of hot buttons and she planned to toy with them.

They walked into the bustling cafeteria and secured their hot drink of choice, then found a table for two in a back corner.

Sam sat against the wall and set her mug on the wood-trimmed Formica table. Mitch slid into the steel-framed hunter green plastic chair across from her.

"So, Sunshine, give me your best shot."

One corner of her mouth curved up. "Suddenly I'm 'Sunshine'?'"

"How can starting off on a lighter note be a bad thing? I'm not stupid."

"No one ever said you were." And the words would never pass her lips. She knew what it felt like to be on the receiving end of that derogatory word. "You're a considerate, caring man."

"No, I'm not. It's a well-known fact that I'm rude and abrasive. In fact, I elevate those particular qualities to artform status."

"Oh, please. If that were true, you wouldn't have made it a point to send that little boy to radiology to have his candy X-rayed after you did his sutures."

"It's a service Mercy Medical offers to the community. Happens every year on Halloween."

"Even so," she said dunking her tea bag in the hot water, "you work awfully hard at being rude and abrasive. I think you care too much."

He blew on his steaming black coffee, then took a sip. "You couldn't be more wrong."

"It's why you get short-tempered when you see someone in pain knowing it could have easily been avoided."

"It's not about caring. I have a zero waste tolerance."

"You say potato, I say po-tah-to."

He frowned. "What does that mean?"

"If you didn't care, your tolerance would be boundless. You, Doctor, are a softie in a Scrooge costume. How appropriate to acknowledge that today. And for the record? When someone says 'thank you' the correct response is 'you're welcome.'"

"I wasn't raised by wolves." The muscle in his jaw clenched as he frowned.

"Speaking of family," she said, "Connor was asking about you."

"Oh? Did you tell him you won't go out on a second date with me?"

"Technically we never had a first date."

What they'd had was sex. If she went out with him again, there was every reason to believe she would sleep with him. Again. Not only was it career suicide, it was a really bad idea personally. Obviously he didn't want to care and she desperately wanted someone to care about her. He was a very bad risk on many, many levels.

"You're a client. It's unprofessional to discuss you with my brother."

"Then I have to assume you brought him up for professional reasons."

She nodded. "The day we had lunch with him, one minute you were on my side, the next your mood took a swing to the dark side. I'd like to know what I said to trigger the sudden shift."

"I have no idea what you're talking about." He said it too fast and too sharply.

"I think you do."

"Oh? Why is that?"

She dunked her tea bag then settled it in her spoon and wrapped the string around it, effectively squeezing most of the liquid from it. "Shakespeare said it best. Methinks he doth protest too much."

"Don't go psychobabble on me, Sam."

"That was literature. But I suppose all the most memorable characters are based in psychology. The thing is, Mitch, you're looking at me now the way you did that day and I can tell by the dark expression in your eyes that something's bothering you. Tell me."

"Do you put this much energy into all your clients?"

No. But the word would never pass her lips. "I do my very best for everyone who comes to me for help."

"That's the thing. I don't think I need help. And you—"

"I'm the one most easily walked all over," she finished.

"You said it, I didn't."

"How we got here doesn't matter. The important thing is that you can benefit from my training and I intend to see that you get something out of our time together."

"You'll get something, too," he said. "A horrible warning about the worst kind of client."

"You're not going to scare me away. Talk like that just makes me more determined to get through to you."

He shook his head. "I'm not worth it, Sunshine. It's time to cut your losses with me."

"I can't." She couldn't tell him that he got to her in a way that had nothing to do with professional and everything to do with personal. It was the worst mistake someone in her position could make. The thing is, caring hadn't been a conscious choice. It just happened. "I've made a commitment to my boss and the company has a lot invested in the success of this contract with the hospital. I'm guessing the hospital has a lot invested in salvaging their employees, not the least of which is the cost of training a replacement."

"Wow, that gave me a warm fuzzy." There was no warmth in his voice or the look he leveled at her.

"I'm not trying to make you feel better," she said. "This is a job. I'm responsible for helping you."

"Don't do me any favors, Sam." His expression darkened like a thunderhead over the mountains when he suddenly pushed his chair away from the table and stood up. "I have to get back to work."

She watched his broad shoulders as he walked away from her and wondered why Mitch didn't simply fire her. Instinctively she knew that he wouldn't tolerate coaching from someone who didn't stand up to him. But meeting him toe-to-toe wasn't getting him to share personal information.

If she were smart, she'd put in her time with him and let it go at that. But she couldn't just go through the motions. Not with him. She'd accused him of caring, which he vehemently denied. It takes one to know one and she cared about him.

And she had to find a way to keep it from being the obstacle that destroyed her career.

Sam's shift was almost over and Mitch was sorry to see it end, even though her reminder that she was responsible for him had touched a nerve. When she left, he wouldn't see her again until their next appointment. She'd made it clear there would be no bending of ethics. Not even a hint of anything personal. That seemed ludicrous considering they'd slept together, but she had him on a technicality since she hadn't been his counselor at the time.

Now he took pleasure in deliberately provoking her and she certainly brightened up the place. But the biggest problem with having her here at the hospital was the distraction of her mouth. When he didn't have to focus on a patient, he couldn't seem to forget how soft and responsive her lips had been. He vividly recalled how good she tasted, how soft her bare skin had felt pressed against him.

They were standing next to the nurses' station while she jotted down a few notes before she left for the day. In her Halloween costume, she was just about the sexiest witch he'd ever seen.

"So, do you have plans tonight?" he asked.

"Yes."

"Costume party?"

"Yes." She glanced at him. "Good guess."

"Have I ever mentioned how helpful my powers of deduction can be in practicing medicine?"

"I don't doubt it."

Watching her make chicken scratches in a notebook reminded him about her dyslexia. He couldn't begin to understand how tough that must have been, yet it hadn't crushed her spirit. She was brimming with enthusiasm and good humor, even when he was surly and irritable, and working at getting a rise out of her. But then, she'd had a lot of practice with that after growing up around Arnold Ryan.

"Here you are."

Mitch turned at the sound of the sultry, female voice. The dark-haired, blue-eyed stunner dressed in tight jeans, tight black sweater and calf-high black boots wasn't looking at him.

Sam smiled brightly. "Fiona. Hi. Thanks for coming by to get me. I'm almost finished."

"Hurry it up. My car is in some poor physician's parking space and if he or she needs it in a hurry, a patient hovering between life and death could be in trouble."

"That would be where I come in," Mitch said.

Frowning, Sam looked from him to the other woman. "I'm sorry. Mitch, this is my sister Fiona. Fee, this is Dr. Mitch Tenney."

Tall, slender Fiona Ryan held out her hand. "Nice to meet you, Doctor."

"Mitch," he said, squeezing her fingers. "Are you going to a costume party?"

"Yes. What was your first clue?" she asked, giving him the once-over.

"It's Halloween. You're here to pick up Sam. She's in

costume and just informed me that she's going to a party." He shrugged. "I connected the dots."

"His powers of deduction are legendary," Sam said wryly. "Don't underestimate him."

"Not a chance." Fiona's eyes sparkled with female interest. "So you're a doctor?"

He nodded. "Emergency medicine."

"As in paramedics, ETA four minutes, GSW to the chest?"

"Gunshot wound?"

"I watch TV." She lifted one shoulder. "The emergency room must be exciting."

He looked at Sam. More than Fiona could possibly know. "There's also the occasional kid in a costume accident. Ignoring flu symptoms for too long. Allergic reactions. You never know what kind of trauma is waiting just around the corner."

"I'm impressed."

He shrugged. "Just the nature of the job."

"You're being too modest. Saving lives is incredibly noble."

It was the ones he couldn't save that haunted him. But he didn't plan on sharing that. "What do you do?"

"I'm an attorney."

"So you're the other Ryan with Upshaw, Marrone, Ryan and Ryan," he said.

"That's right. How did you know?"

"Connor came by for lunch one day," Sam said. "I introduced him to Mitch."

Fiona glanced between them. "I have powers of deduction, too, and I'm guessing Mitch is one of your clients?"

"Yes."

"If only mine were as interesting," she said.

"Be careful what you wish for." Sam clicked her pen closed and flipped the papers back on her clipboard.

"What kind of law do you practice?" Mitch asked.

Fiona shrugged. "A little of this. A bit of that. Corporate mostly."

"Too bad."

"Oh?"

"If you were a trial attorney you'd have the jury eating out of your hand," he said.

"Fiona doesn't have to rely on her looks," Sam snapped. "She's too smart for that."

"I'm sure she is." Mitch didn't miss the irritation in his coach's voice. Did it have anything to do with his premeditated sexist remark or the fact that he was flirting with her sister to deliberately needle her? "But the fact that she's beautiful can only work in her favor."

"People do tend to underestimate me," Fiona agreed. "I used to find it irritating. Why is it men can be hunky and smart, but a woman can't be brainy and beautiful?"

"That's a good question." Mitch leaned against the high counter of the nurse's station. "Obviously a smart girl like you uses all her assets."

"*You* could take lessons." Sam was actually scowling at him. "Oh, that's right. You are taking lessons."

And he had liftoff on the provocation rocket. "I thought we established that I have excellent powers of deduction."

"And if you tacked on some of the charm you're taking out for a spin, you could rule the world," she snapped. "I've been trying to get you to tap into this side of your personality. Who knew my sister could bring it out in less than a minute?"

"Imagine that," he said calmly. "So, Fiona, what are you going to be for Halloween?"

"The cape is in the car." She smiled. "Little Red Riding Hood."

"Watch out for the Big Bad Wolf," he cautioned.

Sam made a scoffing sound. "Wolf alert, Fee. Run far, run fast while there's still time."

"If I didn't know better, Sam, I'd be offended that you believe I have less than honorable intentions."

"You mean you don't?" Fiona glanced at her sister. "That's a real shame."

"Don't we need to get going, Fee?"

Fiona glanced at the watch on her wrist, then smiled at him. "Yes. We're late and I'm in an unauthorized parking space. Nice to meet you, Mitch."

"The pleasure is all mine."

"I'll bring the car around to the E.R. entrance and meet you there, sis."

"Okay." Sam watched until her sister had walked through the double doors.

When she started to walk away without a word, Mitch put his hand on her arm. "Hold it."

"What?"

"Do you want to tell me what made *your* mood swing to the dark side?"

"No."

"You're not jealous, are you?"

"Don't flatter yourself."

"Heaven forbid," he said, holding up his hands. "But I couldn't help noticing that your hostility was showing just a little. Most people wouldn't even be aware of it. But you and I have spent a little time together working on my sensitive side. So…" He shrugged.

Her eyes narrowed and if her face wasn't painted green there would be pink in her cheeks. It took very little to remind him of the night he'd taken her home after her father had made her cry. He'd hated seeing her hurt but couldn't regret that he'd been there for her.

"We've spent time together in a professional capacity," she said, clearly unwilling to acknowledge the personal.

"That's true. But I've come to know your personality a little, just as you've observed me." He studied the expression in her brown eyes and couldn't get a handle on what she was thinking. Crooking a finger beneath her chin, he nudged it up. "What's up with you, Sam? You're looking a little green. Is it possible you're jealous?"

"Not possible. I *am* jealous."

"I see."

And he was glad he wasn't the only one. It was shallow, selfish and stupid. Not to mention a damn waste because this attraction couldn't go anywhere. But he couldn't deny it was there.

"Boys always like Fiona better." Surprise widened her eyes. "Did I say that out loud?"

"Yeah." He straightened her pointy hat. "You're talking about in school, right?"

"I mean now. Whenever we're together boys—men—are drawn to my sister."

"I'm not."

"You were flirting with her," she accused.

"Busted."

She looked confused but that didn't stop her from glaring at him. "If you're not attracted to her, why were you flirting? And badly, I might add."

"Shame on you, Sunshine. That was a low blow."

"Sorry." She sighed. "I don't like being jealous."

"And yet you stood up for her," he pointed out.

"She's my sister. We had our issues growing up but we have a good relationship now."

"Okay."

"I love her." She pulled the brim of her hat lower on her forehead. "I don't expect you to understand the Ryan family dynamics."

"Does love give them the right to walk all over you?" Now he'd said it.

"They don't do that," she protested.

"Maybe not Connor and Fiona. At least not that I've seen. But don't even try to tell me your father doesn't. I was there. What I don't get is why you take it."

"The connection to my family means something," she defended. "Preserving it is important to me."

"You don't owe him your soul."

Her eyes narrowed. "Let me get this straight. The tension between you and your mother is strung so tight the two of you look like you'll snap if you speak for more than two minutes." She tapped her lip. "Oh, and you're divorced. You take some blame, but it's not your fault the marriage couldn't be saved. Do I have it right?"

Those were the facts he'd given her, but that was like diagnosing a brain tumor with nothing to go on but pulse and respiration. There was so much more. The waste of an innocent life—his child—and the lie that preceded it. Marriage kind of implied that a husband and wife made decisions together. Not so much for him and Barbara. That had damaged the marriage beyond hope of resuscitation.

"We're not talking about me."

"And you have no right to talk about me unless your powers of deduction give way to being an expert on commitment, relationships and love. Until that happens, I'd appreciate it if you wouldn't play Little Red Riding Hood and the Big Bad Wolf with my sister."

"Not a problem."

"Okay." She made sure her nose was on straight, then said, "Happy Halloween."

As he watched her walk away, Mitch frowned. Sam had told him off and that turned him on as much as when she was brimming with sweetness and light. Fiona wasn't the sister he was interested in and that was a damn shame. He had the hots for the Ryan who believed that love and commitment went hand in hand with responsibility.

He'd been there, done that, and all he had to show for it now was zero tolerance for waste.

Chapter Eight

Sam walked through the E.R.'s double doors when they whooshed open, then went to the information desk. She was relieved to see Rhonda, the nursing supervisor.

The woman smiled warmly. "Hi, Sam."

"Rhonda." She was too uptight to return the smile. "Is Mitch here?"

"No. As a matter of fact he left early. Why?"

"He didn't show up for his scheduled appointment."

"He probably forgot," Rhonda said.

Sam knew that couldn't be. For the last month they'd been meeting several times a week with field observations thrown in. In that time she'd learned Mitch had a mind like a steel trap and forgot nothing. She went from troubled to worried in a heartbeat.

"Is there a reason he left early?" she asked.

"It's pretty quiet. Now." The plump brunette hesitated.

"What?" Sam implored. "Did something happen."

"This is the emergency room. Something always happens."

"I mean was he too honest? Did he push buttons and stir the pot?"

Rhonda shook her head. "It was just a bad day for him."

"It would help if I knew—"

"You need to ask Mitch."

"If I knew where he was, that's exactly what I'd do. I called the home number on file and his cell, but he didn't pick up, either. I don't even know where to start looking." Sam leaned against the counter, suddenly exhausted as a bad feeling trickled through her.

"If I were you, I'd start looking at Green Valley Ranch."

"The hotel/casino?" When Rhonda nodded, she said, "The place is pretty big. Can you be more specific?"

"The Whiskey Bar. He's mentioned it in passing a couple of times."

"Anywhere else?"

"Besides GVR, here and home are the top two." Her round face took on a curious expression. "Are you going to look for him?"

"Yeah."

"Why?" Rhonda's gaze was direct. "I mean he didn't show up at his scheduled time. It happens. Most people don't go out of their way to find out why. They just charge a missed appointment fee. So what's up?"

"It's part of the Marshall Management Consultants service."

"Then you're practically the only ones on the planet who still make house calls."

Sam ignored that. "Thanks for the information, Rhonda. If he shows up will you ask him to call me?"

"Sure thing."

Sam walked into the parking lot where it was dark and a cold wind was blowing, almost as cold as the dread building inside her. She chirped her car open then slid behind the wheel, started the engine and pulled out onto Mercy Medical Center Parkway. After crossing Eastern Avenue she continued to Paseo Verde and turned right.

When she'd gone looking for Mitch, she hadn't thought

about how it would look. Rhonda was right about her behavior being above and beyond the call of duty. But she had good reason. The reputation of her company was at stake, not to mention her own. She was trying to prove to her father that she was smart. Validation of that fact would come when she was successful. Failure with a client, one who could impact her father's position, was not the way to achieve her career goal.

And if she believed all of that, she could sell herself beach front property in Pahrump. She was worried about Mitch. He wasn't a flake and in her gut she knew something was wrong.

She made a left-hand turn into the parking lot at the Green Valley Ranch Resort, then followed the signs to the parking garage. She parked on the fourth floor, then went straight into the place without taking an elevator. It was like walking into a wall of noise. Her senses were assaulted by the ringing and beeping of slot machines. Garishly lighted games were everywhere. On her left was the food court complete with places offering pizza, hamburgers, wraps and coffee. As she moved farther inside, she spotted signs for the multitude of drink and restaurant choices. After following the arrows, she found the Whiskey Bar and stepped inside.

When her eyes adjusted to the dim light, she looked around. There were places to sit at the bar, with booths around the perimeter and tables scattered throughout. The wood, leather, glass and chrome conveyed an atmosphere of understated elegance and sophistication. For a weeknight in early November, the place was surprisingly full. Her heart sank when she didn't spot Mitch, but she decided to walk through just in case.

And there he was at a booth in a dark corner. All alone. Dressed in a dark T-shirt and black leather jacket, he looked more like a rebel bad boy than a doctor. She moved closer and noticed that in front of him was a glass with clear liquid and a lime.

Sam stopped beside him. "Hi."

He didn't look up and didn't say anything.

"Mind if I join you?" she asked.

"Go away, Sam."

It was the tone in his voice more than the dark, bleak expression in his eyes that made her do just the opposite. She sat in the bench seat across from him. "What are you drinking?"

"None of your business."

If he was drowning his sorrows, she was making it her business. She signaled the cocktail waitress, a pretty blonde in a low-cut top and short skirt revealing long legs encased in black nylons.

"What can I get for you?" she asked with a smile.

"I'll have what he's having," Sam answered.

"Club soda with a twist of lime. Coming right up." She walked away.

It was a relief that he wasn't medicating with liquor. She picked up the cocktail napkin and folded it. "Did you forget that we had an appointment?"

"No."

So not showing up was deliberate. "You've never missed one before."

He met her gaze. "So bill me."

This was getting her nowhere. She'd try another tack. "Aren't you going to ask how I found you?"

"I don't care. If you were smart, you'd lose me again."

"You could have called. Explained that it's been a bad day and rescheduled. I was concerned. This behavior is out of character."

"This is exactly my character—a loner who doesn't count on anyone and that works both ways."

"You're saying no one should rely on you?"

He just looked at her, his mouth pulled tight as the muscle in his jaw jerked.

Sam was worried before, but now she was borderline frightened. He'd been alternately abrasive, rude, heroic and sexy, but never so dark and wounded. It was as if his soul had imploded and she couldn't stand to see him like this.

"Talk to me, Mitch."

"If I'd wanted to do that, I'd have kept the appointment."

"I'm not your coach, now. I'm your friend. Tell my why it was a bad day."

He shook his head and for a moment there was bottomless misery in his eyes. A hard, dark, angry look pushed it away. "Rhonda has a big mouth."

"Not nearly big enough because she wouldn't tell me what happened."

"It doesn't matter."

"I want to help you, but I can't if you won't open up. What was it, Mitch?"

"Just go—"

The cocktail waitress set her club soda with a lime twist in front of her and said, "Anything else I can get you two?"

"No," Sam said. "Thank you."

Mitch watched her for a moment, then looked back. "I'm fine, Sam. Go home."

She toyed with her straw. "Not until I finish my drink."

He glared at her. "You don't even want that."

"You're right. I want you to let me help with whatever is bothering you. And I'm not leaving until you do."

"Then I will," he said.

"I'll follow."

"Damn it, Sam—" His voice was harsh with exasperation. "Go away. Please—"

"No. We can sit here and say nothing. Or you can save us both a lot of time and aggravation and just give it up." She took a sip of her drink. "Why did you have a bad day?"

Their gazes dueled in the silence as he took her measure. Finally he blew out a long breath and said, "I lost a patient."

"I'm sorry. That must be hard. But why was this patient different?"

"What makes you think that?"

"Patients die in the E.R. It happens. Some are too badly injured by the time they're brought in. Sometimes they're just too sick. It's the nature of what you do and you're completely aware of that. But this is the first time I've seen you disappear into your cave. What's different?"

"It was a guy. Late thirties. Drug overdose."

She searched his face and knew there was more. "Why did this one hit you so hard?"

"Because of my brother."

"Your twin?" she asked.

He nodded. "Robbie. We were always close growing up, always friends. But after my dad was killed—"

"Murdered?" She tried to keep her tone normal when she was horrified by that revelation.

"He was a cop. It's how he and my mom met. Robbie and I were ten or eleven. This particular day he was off duty and working an extra job in security at a convenience store when some punks tried to rob it. They shot him and he died on the way to the hospital."

"Oh, Mitch, I'm so sorry."

"Yeah. Me, too." He held his glass and turned it in circles. "He had benefits, but my mom still had to support the family. She wasn't a detective then. Still a patrol cop."

"That must have been hard. After losing your dad, you

must have worried and wondered whether or not she'd come home."

His look was far away, as if he wasn't with her any longer. "Every time she went to work she told me to look after Robbie."

"You were twins. That made you the same age."

"But Mom always said I was the responsible one. When I gave her a hard time, she played the responsibility card, reminded me he was my brother, and I loved him, so it was my job to keep him safe."

He'd told her his brother was dead and she had an idea what was coming. As much as she wanted to fill in the blanks and spare him, there was the danger of him shutting down. He needed to say the words.

"What happened to Robbie?" she asked.

He met her gaze and the pain there was palpable. "He started using. After high school. After I went away to college. He abused drugs for years and eventually died at Mercy Medical Center."

"You weren't on—"

"No."

Her heart went out to him. "It's not your fault, Mitch."

There was irony and self-loathing in his expression. "Then who's to blame? I didn't take care of him. And I didn't save him."

"You're a man. You're human. You're a gifted doctor, but not a miracle worker. Robbie made a choice to take drugs, then became addicted. He couldn't shake it. That's not your fault. You can't blame yourself for that." She could see he wasn't buying it. "You're a doctor and you save lives every day. You need to hang on to that. And remember this—in order to be successful one must learn to surmount a fear every day."

"Spare me the motivational platitudes. I'm not afraid to be a doctor. That's the easy part." His mouth twisted. "Do you know why I specialized in emergency medicine?"

"No. Tell me."

"Because the patients are only in my care for a short time. I'm there for the golden hour. I stabilize them then pass them on for long-term care." He pushed his glass away.

"Someone has to do the job and it takes a special kind of person to handle the pressure you deal with every day."

"But I chose to do it for very specific reasons. Don't you get it, Sam? The message here is that I'm not a long-term kind of guy. I never have been and never will be. In the long term I screw up. You're wasting your time on me."

"It's my time. And I don't happen to agree with you that you're a waste."

She would, however admit to being deflated. He'd just confided a very private, personal pain and it was a break-through in her work. She should be exhilarated; this was *her* "golden hour." But exhilaration was nowhere in sight. It was missing along with any hint of professional pride. What she felt was a deep empathy for what Mitch had experienced and it crossed over into personal territory.

She'd been straddling this line since meeting Mitch, but tonight she'd inched into a danger zone that put all her goals, including career and personal, at risk.

She'd grown up feeling like nothing more than a duty to her stepfather. But she was a woman now and found a need that bordered on desperation to know what it felt like to be loved for herself, for the unique qualities that made her who and what she was.

Why was fate so cruel? What was it about Mitch Tenney that had gotten her heart's attention from the first time she'd seen him?

Forget that he was a client. Forget her professional respon-sibility. It was time to face the fact that she had feelings, intense feelings, for a man who believed loving was another word for obligation. Caring about a client in a personal way was bad enough. Caring about a man who was completely wrong for her was foolish and just plain stupid. The problem was that she simply didn't know how to smarten up.

Mitch followed the red taillights of Sam's practical little import until she turned into her complex. His responsibility to see her safely home was effectively complete. But when the security gates swung shut behind her he suddenly felt the need to make sure she got inside okay.

He turned in and stopped at the keypad and punched in her code, hoping it hadn't changed from the last time he'd been here. Memories of that night were never far from his mind and when the gates opened again, he let out a long breath.

This felt a lot like a B horror movie when some idiot goes into the basement alone and everyone but the idiot knows he's going to get whacked. Mitch knew being here didn't make him the sharpest scalpel in the drawer but he couldn't seem to turn the car around.

He wasn't sure why he was here. One minute he'd been in the bar, brooding and miserable. He was alone and doing a damn fine job of it. Then he'd seen Sam, looking so incredibly sweet, beautiful and concerned. About him. That big heart of hers had compelled her to come looking when he'd stood her up for his appointment. Then, in the bar, he couldn't get rid of her. So he got mad, spilled his guts and still she'd stayed, listening and encouraging. Then she'd said it was getting late and she had to go. She had plans the next day. It had been on the tip of his tongue to ask her to stay, but he didn't. Something got in the way.

In order to be successful one must learn to surmount a fear every day. He was afraid of getting close because love makes you responsible and that was too much to live up to. He wasn't looking for success. He just didn't want to be alone.

So he'd insisted on following her home.

Now he was climbing the stairs to see her into her apartment.

When she heard his footsteps on the walkway, she turned. "I didn't know— You didn't have to do this."

He took the key from her hand just as he'd done the last time. "A gentleman always sees a lady safely home."

The stiff breeze blew strands of hair around her face and he tucked them behind her ears as she clutched her purse in front of her like a shield. When she shivered, he instinctively moved to shelter her from the wind.

"Are you cold?"

"No. Yes," she amended. "You know how it is in Vegas. One day it's eighty degrees, the next it's fifty."

Her voice was all nerves and the idea that he'd made her edgy was extremely satisfying. He wanted to make her as jumpy as she made him. He wanted to dig beneath her cool coach's exterior and find the woman who was jealous when he'd flirted with her sister. Better yet, he'd like to be with the sensuous lady who'd taken him to a place he'd never been before.

"I'd be happy to warm you up." He rubbed his hands up and down her arms.

"Thanks. But it's best if I just go inside. Thanks for seeing me home, Mitch. Good night."

He'd have let her go if there'd been any conviction in the words. She was wearing black slacks and a matching jacket, short and perfectly fitted to her small waist. Beneath it was a silky gold blouse that brought out all the highlights in her big brown eyes. The need to take it off and make her eyes light up for completely different reasons was becoming too difficult to ignore.

"Aren't you going to invite me in for a nightcap?"

Her expression was wry. "Isn't that just the way? I'm out of club soda and fresh lime."

"I can be fresh," he said.

"That's not breaking news."

He leaned a shoulder against the door frame and looked down at her. "I'm shocked and appalled. I do believe my sensitivity coach just insulted me."

"You said it. I simply agreed with you," she countered. "There's a difference."

"I thought you were supposed to spin my behavior into a more positive light."

"And I thought you liked to be right."

"I do," he agreed. "So let me show you just how fresh I can be."

He cupped her cheek in his hand, then lowered his lips to hers. Half-expecting her to back away, he was pleased and surprised when she didn't. He forced himself to go slow, kiss her softly, even though he wanted, with an almost desperate intensity, to pull her into his arms and feel every part of her pressed against him. He ached for her in a way he'd never ached for anyone before.

She swayed toward him and he slid his fingers into the hair at her nape, making the contact of their mouths more firm. He sucked on her top lip then bit down gently, before pressing a light kiss there. When he pulled back and looked down, her eyes were closed and there was a dazed and dreamy expression on her face to go along with her unsteady breathing. The look cranked the blood through his veins and sent it points south, ratcheting up his need.

She was as turned on as he was.

Then the haze faded and she looked distressed. "I—I have to go now, Mitch."

"I'll go with you."

She shook her head. "That's a very bad idea."

The need throbbing through him said otherwise. "You're wrong about that, coach."

"That's exactly why it's not good. You're my client. It's unethical for me to even kiss you, let alone— You know."

He did know. And what he had in mind didn't feel the least bit unethical from where he was standing. If she was using sex to influence him, he could see her point, but that's not what was happening here. He wanted her and he'd bet everything he owned that she wanted him, too. All he had to do was make her see the wisdom of it.

"You mean this?" he asked, lowering his mouth to hers again.

He slid an arm around her waist and pulled her against him, savoring the feel of her breasts pressed against his chest. For the rest of his life he would be grateful that she hadn't worn a coat tonight. He kissed her and when he traced her lips with his tongue, she opened for him and he didn't waste the opportunity. Dipping inside, he caressed the warm sweetness of her mouth. Their tongues dueled in a seductive dance until he thought his chest would explode.

He dropped gentle kisses on her nose, eyes and cheeks, then trailed his mouth across her jaw and down her neck. All the while heat balled in his belly and billowed outward.

Breathing hard, he pulled back. "That didn't feel unethical to me."

"Mitch, I can't—"

He pressed a finger to her lips. "Not what I want to hear."

Why was he letting her get to him? *Letting?* That implied control over his feelings and he so wasn't in control. This *thing* for her just was and if he was as brilliant and worth saving as everyone thought, he'd walk away and never look back. But he couldn't make himself U-turn any more than he could in the car. His life would lose the only light and color in it. If he knew anything it was that life was fleeting and fragile and could disappear in a flash. It was a breeding ground for regrets and he had too many already.

She pressed her forehead to his chest, fighting to suck in air. When she looked up, her eyes were pleading for under-standing. "You're a doctor. If anyone should understand, it's you. I'm ethically bound to maintain my professional distance from a client."

If that was the only thing standing in their way, he had the perfect solution. "Okay, then."

"I'm glad you understand." Regret stood out in her eyes as she turned the knob on her front door and opened it a crack. "I really have to go now—"

"Tell me something, Sam."

"What?"

"Tell me you don't want this. Tell me you're not the least bit interested in me. Not the least bit tempted to throw ethics out the window and burn up the sheets with me." He curved his fingers around her arm and held her gaze. "Tell me that and I'll walk away without looking back. And don't lie to me because you're not very good at it."

She caught her top lip between her teeth. "I can't say that."

"That's what I thought." He let out a long breath. "In that case, you're fired."

In one motion, he pulled her into his arms and inside her apartment then nudged the door closed. Sam reached over his shoulder and twisted the dead-bolt lock. He kissed her until she was breathless and he ached with need.

"I want to see what your bedroom looks like," he said, his voice hoarse.

"Pink."

"What?"

She took his hand and led him past her beige-and-maroon sofa and the kitchen with the copper stuff on the hutch. In the hall she turned right and flipped a switch on the wall. A brass lamp beside the bed lit the room in a golden glow. It was definitely pink, from the roses on the comforter to the sheets beneath. The walls were a soft shade of pink with white crown molding and door. This was a surprise, a contrast from the living room's harvest gold with the one red wall that had given him a hint of the passionate side she kept hidden.

He grinned down at her. "It's a good thing I'm secure in my masculinity."

"A very good thing," she said, sliding her hands over his chest to push off his jacket.

That was all the encouragement he needed. In seconds their clothes were in a heap at the foot of the bed and the sheets were as bare as Sam. Without taking his mouth from hers, he backed her toward the bed.

"Wait," she said.

"What?"

"Do you have— You know." When he stared blankly, she said, "Protection."

He did and automatically answered, "Yes."

Then he reached for the wallet in his jeans to retrieve the condom. The first time she hadn't mentioned it. Of course he hadn't, either, because the blood drained from his head, making rational thought impossible. Later he'd figured she was still on the pill, after her broken engagement.

When he turned back and saw her derriere as she crawled onto the bed, rational thought again drained from his head along with the blood pounding elsewhere.

With protection in place, he slid in beside her and took her in his arms. Her bare breasts burned into his chest and he brushed his palm down her back and over her butt, gently squeezing. She curved a hand over his shoulder, up his neck, then traced one finger along his ear. It was like a bottle rocket going off in his head.

He rolled her onto her back, then leaned down to take the tip of her breast in his mouth. The feel of her skin against his mouth and his hands made him feel as if he'd died and gone to heaven. He turned his attention to her other breast as he slid his hand between her legs, dipping one finger into her feminine warmth. She was as ready as he was and he'd been ready for too damned long.

"I need you, Sam—"

"Ditto," she whispered.

He raised over her, spreading her legs wide with his knee, then pushed gently into her. It was like coming home. He slid his hand between them, and with his thumb found the nub of nerve endings that was the heart of her pleasure. He rubbed it, experimenting with the right amount of pressure until she sucked in a breath and went still, at the same time breathing in a series of harsh gasps that told him she'd found her release.

He thrust in and out until his body tensed. A moment later it felt as if his skull was exploding in the best possible way. When he could move, he rolled to the side, taking her with him wrapped in his arms.

When he could think again, his first thought was that he was going straight to the devil.

His second: hell would be worth it.

Chapter Nine

The next morning Sam put coffee grounds and water into the automatic pot and turned the switch to On. Mitch was behind her, leaning against her cupboards, dressed only in worn jeans zipped but not buttoned, leaving an intriguing expanse of chest and belly exposed. His hair was tousled from sleep and his jaw dark with stubble. The look worked even better than the tuxedo, better than scrubs. Only naked would have been superior to the way he looked right this moment.

She wasn't sure whether to be happy or upset about last night, then decided to go with happy. Career and personal fallout could just wait while she savored the moment. But they had to get one thing straight and it couldn't wait for coffee.

Wearing nothing but a thigh length champagne-colored silk robe, she turned to face him. "You fired me, Mitch, and you can't undo that any more than I can take back going to bed with you. It would be like shutting the barn door after the horse got out. So to speak," she added when the corners of his mouth turned up in a wicked grin.

"Not a problem from my perspective." He met her gaze briefly, then lowered his own to somewhere in the region of her knees.

"So you're willing to finish your coaching sessions with Darlyn?"

"Not a problem from my perspective," he repeated, still staring intently.

"Focus—"

"I am."

"Not on my legs."

"Okay." Slowly his gaze scanned upward then settled on her face. "Not a problem from this perspective, either."

The compliment started a warm glow in her belly that spread until happiness touched her everywhere. Last night had been probably the best night of her life and today was shaping up nicely, too. For this moment in time she wasn't going to wonder about tomorrow. She wasn't going to think about his revelation that he was only into temporary fixes.

She'd known all of that when he kissed her and still she couldn't resist the chance for the pleasure his arms offered.

"Good. Then you can make an appointment with Darlyn to complete your coaching and explain that it's time for a change since you've gone as far with me as you can."

"The best part is that's no lie." Again he grinned the wicked grin that turned her bones to liquid.

He straightened away from the counter and moved toward her, a predator on the prowl. Her heart started racing and she couldn't seem to catch her breath when he crooked a finger and nudged her chin up for a soft kiss. A morning-after endearment.

He looked down and said, "What are my chances for a cup of coffee?"

"Oh." She wasn't exactly sure how long ago the pot had gone silent. "Coming right up."

She opened the white enamel door of the upper cabinet and pulled out two mugs. After pouring the steaming liquid into each, she handed one to him, then put sugar and cream into hers.

"Thanks." He took a tentative sip, then blew into the steam.

"Do you want something to eat? Cereal? Eggs and toast?"

"No bacon?"

She wrinkled her nose. "Can you spell cholesterol, Doctor?"

"Eggs sound good."

"Scrambled or poached?"

"Surprise me," he said.

"I think over easy so you can dip your toast in the runny part. My mother used to make them that way for me, so I could have fun with food."

She pulled out the toaster, omelet pan, bread and eggs, then started cooking.

"What else do you remember about your mother?" Mitch asked, back braced against the cupboards beside her.

She pushed the bread down into the four-slice toaster, then cracked three eggs into the pan. "I have flashes of memory from when it was just the two of us. She was always there for me and I knew how important I was to her. Then she remarried."

"Ryan."

"Yeah." She glanced up and saw his mouth pull tight. "I think I always sensed that I was the worse part of 'for better or worse.'"

"You could never be that."

"Nice of you to say."

"I'm not nice. You know that better than anyone. So it must be the truth."

The sadness she always carried inside her pushed against the boundaries and she fought to keep it back. "I didn't notice so much while my mother was still alive. She always made me feel special." She looked up at him and shrugged. "Then she died and my stepfather was stuck with me."

The toast popped up and she buttered it, then slid the eggs out of the pan onto two plates. "Silverware is in that drawer closest to the table."

Mitch found it and followed her and the food to the dining area. After grabbing two napkins from her pumpkin-colored pottery bowl on the counter, she grabbed the coffeepot and set it on a cow-shaped copper trivet on the table. Then she sat down at a right angle to him.

He ate in silence for several moments, then said, "How did you feel about being adopted?"

"Confused." She held her fork suspended over her plate.

"Why?"

"I don't think it was a conscious thing and I only put it together with the perspective of maturity and hindsight."

"Not to mention your brother's bombshell?" he asked.

"That, too. On a certain level I think I was aware that my father wasn't crazy about me and didn't really want me around. So I was pathetically grateful when he told me he was going to make me his daughter legally." She met his dark gaze. "I didn't know consciously until Connor connected the dots."

"Yeah." He put his fork and knife on his empty plate. "Obviously it was a manipulation to bump the public's perception of him as a swell guy. He legally adopted his dead wife's orphaned child and looked like a hero."

She winced at the harsh assessment, even though it was probably the truth. "Try to see it from his perspective."

"Do I have to?" He pushed his plate away, then refilled both of their coffee cups. "I don't think it's a well-kept secret that I don't think much of him. Never have and never will."

"Okay, then look at it from my point of view. He did the right thing, regardless of his motivation. He gave me a home, clothes, food."

"He gave you criticism and manipulation."

"You just described every parent in the world." She took a bite of toast and chewed thoughtfully. "He's the only father

I've ever known. The dynamic is complicated, but the result is the same."

"And that is?"

"I can't help wanting his love and his respect." She met his gaze. "So much so that I accepted a marriage proposal from a man my father picked out. I never loved Jax, which is probably why he cheated."

"That's just bull." Mitch stood up and anger rolled off him in waves. "If he wasn't happy, he should have manned-up and said so instead of going behind your back. How can you blame yourself for the fact that the creep was unfaithful?"

"The same way you hold yourself responsible for your brother's accidental overdose. It's the way I'm wired." She watched the muscle move in his clenched jaw. "I guess I thought if I married a man approved by my father he would love me."

"Screw that." Mitch jammed his fingers through his already tousled hair. "It was nothing more than an arranged marriage. That went out with hoop skirts and powdered wigs and you should tell him what he can do with it."

She cradled the hot mug between her cold hands. "I can't do that. Don't you see? I got a glimpse of what it's like to have no one to care about you. It's no more appealing now than it was when I was six. It's a risk I'm not willing to take."

"So you put up with all his crap instead—"

There was a knock on her door and Sam started. She automatically glanced at the clock on the microwave over the stove, surprised that it was 10:05. It was Saturday morning and—

"Oh, my God." She stood up.

"What's wrong?"

"Connor. I completely forgot." First Mitch's crisis, and then his kisses had pushed everything else from her mind.

For one moment, she thought about asking Mitch to duck

into the bedroom, but knew he'd never go for that. When there was a second knock, she hurried and unlocked the dead bolt, then opened the door. Her brother stood there dressed in khaki pants and a hunter green sweater with the collar of his shirt poking out. Very preppy. Very proper. And she was in her short, silk robe. So not proper.

So not ready. What with passion, sex and Mitch spending the night, she'd completely forgotten her brother was picking her up this morning. "Hey, Connor."

"Hi, Sam. Someone overslept, I see," he said, glancing at her appearance. He brushed past her and walked into the apartment. His back was to her but she knew when he saw Mitch because his shoulders tensed. "Or not."

She pulled the tie on her robe tighter as she walked around him and stood between the two men who were oozing testosterone like an oil spill from a run-aground tanker.

"Connor, you remember Mitch."

"Yes." His eyes narrowed. "Doctor."

"Ryan." Mitch stood with feet braced wide apart, arms folded over his bare chest. Classic male posturing, which was not helpful for anything.

This was awkward. "I'm so sorry, Connor. I completely forgot about our trip to the art exhibit." She looked up at Mitch. "It's at the Wynn Hotel. A private collection that's on display." She looked up at her brother. "I can be ready in fifteen minutes."

"So," Connor said, not looking at her. "You spent the night with my sister."

"What was your first clue?" Mitch asked.

"It's not a big deal, Connor—"

"You're my little sister. If someone is taking advantage of you, it's a very big deal."

"Mitch isn't doing that," she protested. "It's a long story and—"

"I bet it is," her brother said, never taking his eyes off Mitch. "Sam, you're too trusting for your own good—"

"Sam's a grown woman," Mitch interrupted. "A consenting adult. And, by the way? Where were you when she needed protecting from her sleazebag fiancé?"

"Mitch—" Sam blew out an exasperated breath. Another situation with multiple methods for a peaceful resolution but he went with confrontational. Maybe it was just as well she couldn't be his coach any longer.

Connor took a step forward. "At least he put a ring on her finger and wasn't a one-night stand—"

"Because he was sleeping with every other woman in town," Mitch growled.

"I don't give a rat's ass about him. It's my sister I'm concerned about. Did you think about her. Her reputation? Career? Family?"

"Hello? I'm right here." Sam stepped between them and looked up at Mitch. "It would probably be best if you go now."

His narrowed gaze jumped to her and she could feel the tightly coiled anger mixing with an overabundance of testosterone. She held her breath.

Finally he nodded curtly. "I'll call you."

"Okay. If you want."

"I want."

"Good."

That was a lie. The day that had started out happy just blew up in her face.

Career and personal had just collided head-on and for the first time in her life she was more upset about the personal.

* * *

Two days later, fittingly on Monday morning, Mitch walked into Arnold Ryan's outer office and looked at his beehive-haired assistant in her late fifties. He'd been called to see the administrator and was pretty sure it had something to do with him spending the night at Sam's. Mental note: her brother was a snitch, and news traveled fast in the Ryan family.

Although he admired the fact that Connor was looking out for his sister, the protective behavior also highlighted the differences between them. Mitch had a habit of letting down the ones he loved. Connor, on the other hand, was the guy in the white hat, riding the white stallion hell-bent for leather to rescue damsels in distress. Even if that meant ratting out his sister.

From the outer office where Mitch stood looking out floor-to-ceiling windows, there was a good view of Mercy Medical Center's serenity garden. Hunter green carpet covered the floor and wood-framed chairs in a lighter shade were scattered around the small room.

"May I help you?"

Mitch moved to the desk where the nameplate read Jennifer Pinto. "I'm here to see him."

"One moment, Dr. Tenney."

"Thanks."

Her blue-eyed gaze narrowed slightly behind her wire-rimmed glasses as she picked up the phone. "Dr. Tenney is here to see you, Mr. Ryan." She nodded and said, "Go right in."

He started to say thanks, then thought better of it. This interview hadn't been his idea, but apparently Sam had planted the seed for the simple rules of sunshine, and it was beginning to bear fruit.

He opened the door and walked in. Ryan sat behind a big desk and the dark wood looked elegant and pricey. Carpet was the same as the waiting room, as were the two chairs situated on it in front of the desk. Behind him was a narrow table holding a series of family photographs. Mitch recognized Fiona, Connor and Sam. In the center of the grouping was a glamour shot of a beautiful woman who looked a lot like Sam. He'd bet his favorite stethoscope that was Catherine Mary Ryan, Sam's mom.

"Dr. Tenney," Ryan said, "thanks for responding so quickly to my message."

Reading between the lines, it was clear he was implying Mitch had hurried in because he was intimidated by the perception of power. It was a testament to Sam's coaching that he didn't tell this arrogant ass to stuff a sock in his summons.

"The E.R. was quiet."

Ryan held out a hand. "Have a seat, Mitch."

"So what did you want to see me about?" he asked, rounding the chair on the left and lowering himself into it.

"The status of your medical group and their contract to staff the E.R."

"What about it?"

"The continuation of your services is predicated on your completing prescribed management coaching."

"I'm aware of that," Mitch said.

"It's come to my attention that your coach has become, shall we say, more than a coach."

He could see where the guy was going and kicked himself for putting her in a tight spot. Even in the heat of passion when he'd refused to see obstacles and kept his eyes on the prize—on her—she'd maintained her professional integrity. All he'd been able to think about was how good she felt in his arms. How soft and sweet the taste of her lips. How fast he could make her his. Even as turned on as she was, Sam had taken responsibility for the fact that kissing a client was unethical. Thanks to her there was wiggle room on this issue.

"Sam is no longer my coach."

"Oh?"

He knew that was an interrogation technique designed to elicit information and he wasn't biting. Mitch stared at him without answering.

After several moments, Ryan cleared his throat. "So, you're saying that you terminated Samantha?"

"It was a mutual decision."

Sort of. She hadn't argued with him. Mostly because he'd deliberately kept her mouth occupied with his mouth. Not until the next morning did she bring up the subject, while he'd been preoccupied remembering the second time he'd made love to her and the way she'd wrapped her shapely legs around his waist while he was buried deep inside her.

"I take it that you've come to see what I've known all along."

"Which is?" Mitch asked.

"That the management coaching program is a waste of your time and a useless drain on the hospital budget." He leaned back in his chair and folded his hands over his flat abdomen. The guy was in great shape. "I've tried to tell Samantha as much, but she insists that a great deal of good can be accomplished."

"Problems become opportunities when the right people join together," Mitch said softly, remembering the picture of the bridge in Sam's office.

"Yes." Ryan nodded. "But there are problems and there are problems."

"You got that right. Pick one."

"My daughter's choice of profession. I believe that's what you're referring to. And I'm guessing that you've recognized the counseling—"

"Coaching," Mitch amended.

"Whatever." Ryan made a dismissive move with his hand. "Clearly you see it as the nonsense it is."

"That's where you're wrong." Mitch stood and looked down at the guy. "If it was nonsense, I would have stopped listening to you five minutes ago. Hell, I'd have ignored the message to come for this interview altogether."

"Are you saying my daughter actually made a difference in your attitude?"

"That's what I'm saying." He folded his arms over his chest. "She's very good at her job."

"It was my understanding that you were opposed to seeing someone for conflict resolution training."

He'd been opposed to having his back against the wall and being forced into it. There was a difference. "I'll admit that I was initially reluctant."

"And now?"

Mitch sent him a pointed look. "I can see the benefits of learning techniques to handle difficult people."

"Does this change in attitude have anything to do with the fact that you're sleeping with my daughter? And that by doing so you've jeopardized her career—such as it is?"

Mitch didn't like this guy. Some of it was about implementing hospital policies that were a waste of time, effort and money. But that was business. Now he just didn't like him on account of the way he put Sam down at every opportunity. And that was personal.

"Your daughter is an incredibly bright, sweet, optimistic woman who is good at what she does."

"Samantha is naive and needs someone to look out for her. It's a father's job to make certain his daughter is secure and well-taken care of."

"You feel responsible for her?"

"Of course." He frowned. "My late wife left her in my care and I take that very seriously."

"To the point where you pick out the man she'll marry even if the guy is a cheating bastard?"

Ryan sat up straight. "What are you talking about?"

"Jax Warner. Sam broke it off because she caught him with another woman."

Barely suppressed fury swirled in his eyes. "Samantha would have told me if that was the truth. She said it was a mutual, amicable decision."

"She kept the ugly details to herself to protect you. If you really cared about her, you'd never have used her like that. You'd never exploit her need to be loved and manipulate her into a relationship that works for you but made her miserable."

Arnold Ryan stood up and met his gaze. "How dare you judge me?"

"I dare because—" Mitch stopped because he didn't know why he was facing this guy down. Maybe it was the underdog thing. He couldn't stand to see anyone get picked on.

"What is the nature of your relationship with my daughter, Dr. Tenney?"

Good question. One he didn't plan to discuss with this guy. At least not in depth. "We're friends."

"And does your friendship include sleeping with Samantha?"

"None of your business."

The man glared daggers for several moments. "Then I'll tell you what is my business, Doctor. Whether or not your employment is continued here at Mercy Medical Center."

"And it's my job to save lives. I'm very good at my job."

"Let's be clear, Doctor."

"Let's," Mitch echoed.

"If you screw up just once, I won't lift a finger to salvage your job. In fact it would give me great pleasure to bring you down. Standing behind Samantha will not save your career, not in my hospital. If you shoot your mouth off again, for any reason, don't make the mistake of believing I'll intercede on your behalf because you slept with my daughter."

Mitch was fuming and tried his best not to let it show when all he wanted to do was deck this guy. This man had set his daughter up with a womanizing loser, claiming the idiot would take care of her. Now he'd managed to make it appear that he was a noble father looking out for his daughter. In fact, he'd just said Mitch wasn't good enough to lick the bottom of her shoes. On top of that, he'd implied Sam could only attract a man who needed her as a career insurance policy.

He stared at Ryan for a long moment, then said, "Understood."

The single word was spoken through gritted teeth. If Sam's coaching wasn't working, his response would have been far less civilized. And before he made a mockery of her work, he turned and walked out of the office.

Damn the man. Who the hell was he to dictate?

He kept using Sam's feelings to manipulate her. The fact that Sam was afraid of not having anyone to love her worked to his advantage. And Mitch was trying his damnedest not to care. He really needed to shut down his feelings because caring about someone led to responsibility. He should be grateful the guy had given him a reality check. He knew he should take the advice and walk away from her.

For his own sake.

But mainly for hers.

Mitch was the wrong man for her and it was the only thing he and Ryan agreed on.

Chapter Ten

After leaving the administrator's office, Mitch went back to work, dealing with victims of a three-car accident on the Fifteen freeway. At least he could focus on something besides how much he wanted to tell Arnold Ryan exactly what he could do with his ultimatum.

He went from one trauma bay to the next, examining the patients. Fortunately no one had been hurt too badly except the guy who thought he was an Indy 500 driver staying one car length in front of the cops. After stabilizing him, the cops transferred the idiot to University Medical Center, where he'd be under armed guard. The police officer who'd managed to cut him off before he'd killed someone had been shaken up and was waiting in the E.R. for a bed upstairs. He was being kept overnight for observation. A parade of police officers had come in and out, supporting one of their own.

Mitch looked up from writing his notes and saw his mother coming through the double doors. As if his day couldn't get any worse.

She glanced around, saw him and walked over, her confident stride eating up the distance. In her black jacket and matching slacks, she looked like a police detective. She also looked tired and he wondered if she really projected cop vibes or he saw her that way because it was easier.

Ellen stopped beside him. "Hi, Mitch."

"Mom." He tapped his pen on the desk. "I guess you're here to see Officer Morrow."

Worry swirled in her blue eyes as she nodded. "How is he?"

"Without breaching patient confidentiality I can tell you he's a very lucky guy."

"Is that medical speak for he's going to be okay?"

He pointed at her. "I bet you're an excellent detective."

"And I bet you're a good doctor. Morrow was in very good hands."

That was the closest she'd come to paying him a compliment in longer than he could remember. It felt good. Took some of the sting out of his face-to-face with Ryan. The bastard.

He really didn't much care what the guy thought of him, but Sam was hungry for her father's respect, acceptance and love. It was possible that Mitch was also ticked off at himself for putting her in a compromising situation.

"Mitch? Are you okay?"

He lifted his gaze to his mother's. "Yeah. Sorry. I was just thinking about something."

"Then I won't keep you. If you'll point me in the right direction, I'll go see Morrow."

"Okay." He half turned and said, "Through those double doors. Trauma bay two. He'll be going upstairs as soon as there's a bed. That shouldn't be long if you want to wait—"

She shook her head. "I'm on my lunch break. I was in the area and just wanted to say hi and see how he's doing."

Mitch flashed on memories of her stopping by on her breaks to look in on him and Robbie. He'd always chafed at having to be responsible for his brother, but his mother's love for them had never been in question. Someone from Las Vegas Metro was always looking out for them and certainly Detective

Tenney was behind that. Neither he nor Robbie could sneeze without her knowing. If anything, she'd been too protective.

Mitch realized that with all their issues, and they were numerous, he'd never questioned his mother's love for him. Not the way Sam doubted being loved.

He remembered the words from the wall of her office. Be a bridge. Maybe this was an opportunity. And he decided to take out for a spin what she'd taught him. It was a three-step approach.

Ellen glanced at the door, then back at him. "Thanks for the info, Mitch. And for taking good care of Morrow. I'll talk to you soon. About Thanksgiving," she added, starting to turn away.

"Wait, Mom."

She stopped. "What's up?"

He remembered Sam talking about data gathering as a method to curtail and resolve conflict in an effective, non-confrontational way. It's not touchy/feely, she'd said. One simply asked questions, gathered data and listened. Don't respond with a viewpoint because that sets up a situation where one or both parties become defensive and start counterattacking. So he had to ask something.

"Was it hard for you when Dad was killed?" It was the first thing that popped into his head.

She looked surprised and that didn't happen often. "Yeah. Real hard."

"How come you never remarried?"

"Aside from the fact that no one asked?" she said, trying to deflect the question.

Sam had told him he did that, tried to distract when the questions touched a nerve. Data gathering. Questions. Keep her talking. "No one asked?" he urged.

"That's not exactly true." Ellen blew out a breath and fixed her gaze on something just over his shoulder that she wasn't really seeing. "At first I had my hands full. With Robbie. You. Working and keeping everything as normal as possible."

"At first? Then what?"

A skeptical look slid into her eyes. "You don't really want to hear this, do you?"

"Yeah."

"Why now?"

So, she was data gathering, too. Duh. She was a detective. Questions were her bread and butter.

He shrugged. "Let's just say I've been getting in touch with my feminine side. So tell me how it was after you kept everything normal."

"There was no such thing as normal for me after your father died. Jason Tenney was the only man I ever loved. One day he was there, the next he was gone. But there were two boys to raise and they were counting on me. It was the alone part that was the hardest."

He knew all about alone.

Trying to avoid it had gotten Sam in hot water with her family and he regretted that, but he just hadn't been able to let her go that night. His mother had had no choice about letting his father go.

"Do you still miss him?" Mitch asked.

Her small smile was incredibly sad. "Every day."

"So you don't date?" Again the words popped out of his mouth and he felt like he was living in an Oprah show.

"I go out every once in a while," she said with a shrug.

"Nothing serious?"

This time there was a hint of humor in her smile. "What are you? My father?"

"Hardly." He smiled, too. "Just curious."

"You get that from me," she said.

Who had he inherited the selfish gene from? He'd carried around a lot of anger at Ellen. Forcing him to be responsible for his brother had rubbed him the wrong way as a kid. When they grew into men, he'd fought a losing battle to save his twin from the addiction that was slowly killing him and Mitch would carry the guilt of that failure to his grave. But he'd never once thought about how hard his mother's life had been without his dad. How lonely and sad she must have felt as she went about being a single mother who worked on the police force while being responsible for raising twin boys.

He wished now that he could have done something to make her life easier instead of being sullen and resentful. So much for step one of data gathering. Step two was asking if there was anything else he needed to know and a promise to give it more thought. He figured he probably had more than enough to think about. Step three was proposing a solution at the next meeting. He'd worry about that another time. Still, this was progress.

Would Sam be proud of him? He hoped so.

His mother glanced at the watch on her wrist. "It's getting late. I've got to run."

"I didn't mean to keep you so long. Sorry."

"Don't be. This was good." She hesitated just long enough to let him know it wasn't comfortable, then opened her arms and gave him an awkward hug.

He responded. It was rusty but that was okay. "It was nice to see you, Mom."

"You, too. Maybe next time it will be under more pleasant circumstances."

"Yeah."

"Maybe Thanksgiving. I could cook."

"I'd like that."

She didn't look quite as tired as when she'd walked in. "We'll talk soon."

"Okay."

She nodded, then went through the double doors to the trauma bay where her fellow cop was being cared for. It was weird. That had actually gone pretty okay thanks to his conflict counselor. And he'd given her such a hard time in the beginning. If Sam hadn't been Sam would he have listened to her at all?

Problems become opportunities when the right people join together.

The good feeling faded when he remembered what her father had said. He wasn't the right man for her. Ryan knew it and so did Mitch.

Sam left her father's office and fought down nausea and the uneasy feeling that followed. Her period was late, but it was probably because of all the stress in her life. Mitch. Now her father had insisted on seeing her. The meeting hadn't been especially pleasant. But why should this one be different?

He didn't think much of Mitch. And Mitch had made it clear he didn't think much of her father. Or her, for that matter, for putting up with what he called her father's crap. The criticism and manipulation.

It was true, she realized. Using the fact that she wanted him to love her, Arnold Ryan had a major influence on who she saw socially and had just revealed his dislike of the man she was seeing.

Sort of seeing.

Sam wasn't exactly sure what they were. She was no longer his coach. She'd slept with him more than once and could be…

She shook her head. It was only the first time that they didn't use protection. No way would the fates be so cruel to her.

"Hey, Sunshine."

She looked up and saw Mitch coming toward her. Her stomach jumped. It had nothing to do with nausea and everything to do with being happy to see him. She hadn't realized how much she'd been hoping for this until he was right there in front of her.

"Mitch."

He stopped beside her and looked down. "Did you just have a meeting with your father?"

"Yeah."

"Want to have lunch with me in the doctor's dining room?"

She tilted her head as she studied him. "This is getting to be a habit." As was the way she couldn't stop thinking about him. How did that happen in such a short time?

"Is that a yes or no?"

"It's an 'I don't think it's a good idea.'"

He slid his hands into the pockets of his white lab coat. "Because Daddy told you to stay away from me?"

"What makes you say that?" she asked, glancing at the closed door behind her.

"Because he and I had a friendly little chat."

Her eyes widened. "What?"

"He sent for me. I showed up. On time. He said some things. I said some things." His mouth thinned for a moment as his jaw jerked. "You'd be proud of me for what I kept to myself."

"Oh, God—"

"Seriously. We put our cards on the table and have a better understanding because of it."

She wasn't sure what that meant, wasn't sure she wanted to. "I think he knows we—" She pointed to him, then herself, then back and forth a couple more times. "You know— We, had umm—"

He leaned over and whispered in her ear, "Sex?"

"Yes."

"He did not get independent confirmation of that fact from me."

"Me, either," she said quickly, cheeks burning.

"So what did you tell him?"

She sighed. "Mostly I just listened. And he managed to get a shot or two in about how management coaching was a waste of time."

"On the contrary," he said. "Thanks to your time, efforts and expertise, along with specific behavioral modification strategies to resolve conflict—"

"Are you making fun of me?"

"Absolutely not." He held up his hands. "What I'm trying to say is that because of you I didn't pop him in the nose even though he deserved it."

"Thank goodness."

That would only have made things worse and Mitch would probably have lost his job. Not to mention that her father wouldn't have hesitated to press assault and battery charges and any other charges he could come up with.

"So, don't I deserve the pleasure of your company for playing nice?"

He thought her company was pleasurable?

"And," Mitch added, grinning wickedly, "wouldn't you just love to thumb your nose at the old man? Right under his nose since the doctor's dining room is just down the hall."

It was the sinful grin that swayed her to the dark side. She'd been doing a convincing job of resisting his charm until he laid that on her.

She smiled back and after the morning she'd had it was a miracle. "Okay, Doctor. Lead me into temptation."

"When opportunity knocks…" He took her hand and tucked it into the bend of his arm.

They passed the door to her father's office and continued on to the dining room, which looked pretty much the same as the last time she'd been here. Thanksgiving holiday decorations were up—signs, turkeys, pilgrims, horns of plenty. In the small vase on each peach-colored tablecloth an arrangement of mums in shades of yellow, rust and orange. Several people were scattered around the room.

She took a tray and followed Mitch past the steam table. The smell of food didn't make her stomach feel any better so she decided on chicken noodle soup and crackers. And a piece of pumpkin pie. His plate was piled with turkey, dressing, mashed potatoes, gravy and green beans. After getting a mug of hot water and a tea bag, she followed him to a table in the far corner.

When they were settled at a right angle to each other, he looked at her food, then met her gaze. "Don't tell me you're on a diet."

"No. Just not very hungry."

He looked concerned. "Are you okay?"

"Yeah. Just a little tired, I guess." There was no point in sharing her stomach issues. The last thing she wanted was more stress about her family situation.

"Not worried about your father?"

"No," she lied. How like Mitch to see straight through her.

He took a bite of turkey and chewed thoughtfully. "When I saw you in the hall, you were looking awfully serious about something. Want to talk about it?"

Not even for money. Her period was late. If she stopped thinking about it, it would come.

"Why don't we talk about your successful use of coaching techniques?" she suggested.

"With your dad?" He scooped up a forkful of mashed potatoes and ate it. "Mostly I kept my temper in check, kept my mouth shut and left before I exploded."

"So there was no newly acquired skill involved in your success?"

"Not then."

That implied he had employed some kind of plan at some point in time. "When?"

"I saw my mom this morning. Right after the face-to-face with your dad."

She moved her spoon around in the soup and took a small bite of cracker instead. "You're really having a good day, aren't you?"

He looked up and settled his gaze on her face. One corner of his mouth turned up. "I am now."

Warmth pooled in her belly, then spread outward, clear through her. If the lights were out, she was sure she'd glow in the dark.

"So, tell me what happened," she suggested.

"She was here to see a cop involved in a high-speed chase. Nothing serious, but Las Vegas Metro supports their own," he explained. "Anyway, I was thinking about you—"

"Oh?" The word popped out, meant to encourage elaboration. It was stupid. She tried very hard not to read anything into his revelation. Anything personal, she amended. Just because they'd slept together didn't mean he owed her promises of forever.

He smiled. "I was thinking about data gathering and decided to try it out on my mom."

"Did anything positive come out of the conversation?"

"That was step one. I'm still thinking about what she said."

"Step two," she clarified.

He nodded. "And moving on to step three is looking pretty good, which is something I never would have expected."

"I'm so glad it helped, Mitch."

"Be a bridge." He shrugged.

"Good for you."

He set his fork down on his plate. "So, your father is wrong about what you do. If you ever need a reference—"

"I just want you to complete your sessions at Marshall Management."

"Will do."

His praise meant a lot to her. He would never admit as much, but in the beginning he was as skeptical as her father. It was good to know he saw some positive results in the work they'd been doing. And now the silence grew between them.

Looking around, she searched for a neutral topic of conversation. The decorations on the wall gave her one. "Can you believe it's almost Thanksgiving?"

"Time flies when you're having fun," he said. "What are you thankful for this year?"

She looked around. "I'm thankful for influential friends who get me into all the right places."

He laughed. "Glad to be of service."

"What are you thankful for?" she asked, taking a forkful of her pie.

"Besides you?" He looked at her and his eyes took on an intensity that got her attention.

Her heart hammered against the wall of her chest and it was almost painful. Surely he could hear. "I was just doing my job."

"Was it your job to track me down when I missed my appointment?" His gaze was probing.

"Sure, I—"

"No fibbing. I don't know anyone who makes house calls, let alone does search and rescue like you did."

"Glad to be of service," she said, echoing his words.

"You definitely were," he agreed.

Past tense. Because their professional association was over. That thought opened up a sad sort of emptiness inside her. Now she had no reason to see him, couldn't look forward to an appointment. Nothing to brighten her day. That reaction was reason enough to sever the connection even if they hadn't slept together.

She looked at his empty plate. "I guess the food was pretty good."

"Yeah. It's as close to home cooking as I get."

"What do you do for meals when you're not working?" she asked, setting her elbow on the table and her chin in her hand as she studied him.

"Take-out. Microwave."

"That's just sad."

"What are you gonna do?" he said with a shrug.

"Learn to cook."

"I don't think so." He shook his head.

"Cooking is very relaxing." She took another bite of her pie, savoring the creamy pumpkin, spices and whipped cream flavors mixing together.

"I'd rather play hopscotch on the freeway." He met her gaze. "Are you a good cook?"

"Come to my place for Thanksgiving and you'll find out." For just a moment she wondered if she'd said that out loud, then the thoughtful, semi-shocked expression on his face answered the question. "That is, if you don't have plans."

"Nothing definite. My mother mentioned something about getting together."

"She's welcome to come, too," Sam offered. "In the interest of full disclosure, I should warn you that my family will be there."

"Including your father?" A dark, dangerous, rebellious sort of look settled in his blue eyes.

"Yes."

"Won't he disapprove?"

"Probably. But he can just suck it up. Or leave. I'm free to invite whomever I want. It's my house and my party."

He thought for a moment, then said, "There's nothing I'd like better than watching Arnold Ryan suck it up."

"Okay, then," she answered, ridiculously happy that he'd agreed to come.

She suspected he'd accepted the invitation more to mess with her father than anything else, but she didn't care. Right then the prospect of spending the holiday with Mitch—the expectation of spending any time with him—was far too appealing.

It wasn't until later, when the glow faded, that she realized his answer to her invitation had been far too important to her.

Chapter Eleven

The last time Mitch had been to Sam's apartment her brother Connor had practically caught them doing the deed and he'd been braced to defend himself. Today was Thanksgiving and he was prepared to defend her—from Arnold Ryan if necessary.

Her dining table was set for six with floral-patterned china, silverware and crystal on a beige- and rust-colored cloth shot through with gold threads. An arrangement of yellow roses and orange mums was set in the middle with little boy-and-girl pilgrim candle holders on either side.

He and his mother had been there for about twenty minutes and so far the tentative truce between him and her brother was holding. Sister Fiona was friendly without flirting and Mitch figured Sam had given a three-step holiday behavior seminar to her siblings. Introductions had been made, beverages handed out and his mom was engaged in a spirited cops-versus-lawyers discussion with the Ryan-and-Ryan half of the Upshaw-and-Marrone firm.

So far her father was a no-show and he wondered if the spirit of full disclosure had extended to him. Did he know Mitch would be there and was deliberately staying away? Although he didn't think the guy was worth worrying about, he knew how important the relationship was to Sam and wondered if he should have turned down her invitation.

The thing was, he was awfully glad she'd asked him to be here. Since firing her, he'd spent a lot of time coming up with excuses to spend time with her. Loose and unclear worked best for him. Running into her at the hospital. Dropping by her office after a counseling session. A friend having him over for a holiday dinner.

He walked into her kitchen, where she'd just finished mashing potatoes and set them on the warming tray until the turkey was ready.

"So," he said, "your brother doesn't look like he wants to rip my head off."

"He still wants to," she said cheerfully. "He's just pretending to be nice because it's a holiday."

"You had a talk with him, right?"

"Pretty much," she confirmed. She glanced into the other room. "Did it take much convincing to get your mom here?"

"No. She likes you," he said.

"She only met me for a minute."

"It was enough." How could anyone not like Sam? he thought. "Can I get you some wine?" he offered.

"I'd love it. I admit to being a little tense. This is the critical time in dinner preparation." Her look was wry. "Not unlike the golden hour when *you* first get a patient in the E.R. and start the battle to save a life."

"How do you figure? Your bird is already a goner."

"But if his sacrifice is going to mean anything, the chef has to intervene at just the right moment in the cooking process. Not too soon, not too late, otherwise the meat is raw or tough as shoe leather." She shrugged. "It's the critical moment."

"I thought you said cooking was relaxing."

"It is. But not on Thanksgiving."

"Point taken. Where's your glass?" He uncorked the open bottle of red wine beside him. "Obviously this is just what the doctor ordered right in the nick of time."

Just starting to reach into the cupboard, she stopped. "On second thought, maybe I better not. It's not a good idea for the cook to get tipsy."

"One won't hurt."

"I better pass."

It wasn't her refusal that got his attention, but the sudden uneasiness in her manner that made him wonder if there was something going on with her. That and she wouldn't quite meet his gaze.

"Are you all right, Sam?"

"Fine," she answered just a little too quickly, her smile a little too bright. She opened the oven, then basted the bird as she said, "I just want to get dinner on the table. Then I can relax."

"What can I do to help?" he asked.

"Nothing at the moment. But at the last minute I'll need you on the trauma team." She leaned back against the counter beside him.

"Done."

"And thanks for bringing the pie." She smiled. "I'm guessing you didn't make it."

"Good guess. I did everyone here a favor and bought it."

"I cook, but baking is out of my league. I planned a frozen pie. Well, it's not frozen now. I heated it last night. The one you brought looks wonderful."

"I got it from a wonderful pie place." He glanced into the living room and saw his mother laugh at something Connor said. "Mom seems to be having a good time."

Sam looked over, then up at him. "I'm glad she came."

"Speaking of parents—Shouldn't your father be here by now?"

She took a quick look at the digital clock on the microwave over the oven. "Yes."

"In the spirit of full disclosure," he said, echoing her words, "did you tell him I'd be here?"

"Yes. And I made it clear that your mother would be joining us, too."

"I can imagine how that went over," he said.

"He's welcome to be here and he knows that."

He looked at the shadows in her eyes and wanted to chase them away, especially because it was his fault they were there. He'd pushed her into shaking things up. But what right did he have to do that to her?

"I shouldn't be here," he said.

"That's where you're wrong." She put her hand on his arm. "The thought of you nuking Thanksgiving dinner was just too awful to contemplate. If my father chooses not to be here, he'll miss out on all the fun—"

There was a knock on the door. Since Fiona was closest, she opened it. "Hi, Daddy."

"Fiona." Arnold Ryan walked in and looked around. "Connor."

"Dad." The two men shook hands. "This is Ellen Tenney, Mitch's mother. She's a homicide detective with Las Vegas Metro."

Ryan held out his hand. "It's a pleasure to meet you, Ellen."

"Same here." Her tone was neutral, but she stared her cop stare. Probably because of the things Mitch had said.

Sam came out of the kitchen to greet him with a hug. "Hi, Dad. Can I take your coat?"

"Yes." He shrugged off his expensive brown suede jacket

and handed it to her after looking around her apartment. "Thank you, Samantha. I always forget how small this place is. And how eclectic your decorating taste is."

In less than a minute he'd managed to take the roses out of Sam's cheeks. That seriously ticked Mitch off and he wanted to tell the guy what he could do with his opinion. It might make him feel better, but it wouldn't help her.

For Sam's sake he had to make nice and forced himself to hold out his hand. "Happy Thanksgiving, Mr. Ryan."

The man only paused a moment before taking it. "Doctor."

The average person wouldn't have noticed his hesitation, but Ellen Tenney wasn't average. She'd built a successful career on reading people.

When the Ryans had moved away, she whispered to Mitch. "I like Connor and Fiona."

"Yeah. They're okay," he said.

"I'd bet my LVPD shield that they take after their mother." He laughed. "No comment."

"Sam seems like a nice girl." Ellen sipped her white wine.

Nice didn't do justice to Sam. Sweet. Sunny. Sexy. No way was he telling his mother that. "Yeah, she is."

Fortunately the turkey was done soon after and a flurry of last-minute preparations eased the tension. Ever the diplomat, Sam asked her father to carve the bird, then put the platter of meat on the table and directed everyone to their seats. Fiona helped her set out mashed potatoes, gravy, stuffing, cranberry mold and green bean casserole. With her father at one end of the table and her at the other, closest to the kitchen, Mitch was on Sam's right, with Fiona on his other side as a buffer. Connor was between Ellen and his father. Sam had given the seating arrangement careful thought, he noted. Keeping him and her father apart.

When all the food had been passed and plates filled, Fiona

raised her glass and made a toast. "To my sister, Sam. Thank you for dinner. And for being my sister."

"That was sweet, Fee," Sam said.

Everyone clinked glasses and murmured agreement, then sipped before digging into the food. Mitch noticed that Sam set her wineglass down untouched.

"Isn't this the part where we all tell what we're thankful for?" Connor asked, forking up a bite of gravy-covered stuffing.

"I'm thankful for you reminding me," Sam said.

"No fair being thankful for family," Connor warned. "And we should hear from honored guests firsts. Ellen, you go. What are you grateful for?"

His mom chewed on a piece of white meat for a moment, then swallowed. "Is it a Ryan family rule that I can't be thankful for my son?"

"Of course you can," Sam answered warmly. "My brother was just kidding."

"No, I wasn't," he chimed in. "That's too easy."

"There's nothing easy about family," Mitch said, meeting his mother's gaze around the tall candle between them.

"There's nothing more precious, either," Sam said.

Ellen sent her a measuring look. "I agree. Those of us who have lost a loved one appreciate things just a little more."

"Isn't that an occupational hazard?" Arnold Ryan asked.

"On the police force there's always a higher level of awareness," Ellen agreed. "It's a blessing and a curse. Detectives not so much. But the men and women on patrol, they're called peace officers for a reason, live with the threat every time they come to work. We always hope nothing happens."

"But if it does, we're grateful for Mitch in the E.R.," Sam said, looking at him.

Leave it to her to find a silver lining at the same time she pulled him into the conversation and told her father he was wrong. Anyone looking at the expression on her face would believe he was a hero. But he knew better.

He also knew she was pushing the food around her plate but not much was going into her mouth. When her father monopolized the conversation at the other end of the table he leaned over and asked her, "Are you okay?"

"Of course," she said. "Why?"

"You're not eating."

She looked down, then back at him. "Did you see the way my plate was piled? No way could I eat it all."

"It's delicious. You're a pretty good cook, Sunshine."

"Thanks." She took a bite of mashed potatoes, then cut a piece of turkey and ate it.

When second helpings were downed and everyone declared themselves completely stuffed, Sam asked, "Anyone for pie?"

The groans were answer enough and she directed that plates be passed down to her. When that was accomplished, she stood to carry them into the kitchen.

Mitch put his hand on her arm. "I'll get that."

"It's not necessary."

"You cooked. I'll fetch and carry." He stood and picked up the pile, then walked around her.

She followed him and started to stack the empty plates in the dishwasher. "Thanks."

"Don't mention it." He folded his arms over his chest. "What I would like you to mention is what's wrong. And don't tell me nothing. This is me."

She looked up quickly. "I—I guess I'm just tired. Maybe a little stressed about this gathering."

"I understand that. But it's going well. You're sure there's nothing else?"

She looked away. "Don't worry about me."

But that was just it. He did worry about her. About her health. About how the rest of her family treated her. Whether or not she was happy. The whole nine yards was fodder for his worry, he realized. That wasn't supposed to happen to him. From worry it was a hop, skip and jump to caring. After that was commitment. The thought didn't make him happy, because that was not something a short-term guy like himself could ever be thankful for.

Mitch leaned back against Sam's kitchen counter as he hand-dried a crystal wineglass. After everyone else went home he'd stayed behind to help clean up, and she was glad. Cooking holiday dinner had never taken so much energy before and she was tired to the bone. On top of that, she just liked having him around. It was going to come back and bite her big time, but of all the things she was thankful for this year, he was at the top of her list.

Sam rinsed another glass and set it out on the dish towel beside the sink. "So tell me why you didn't find it necessary to see your mother safely home."

"She's a cop." He held the glass up to the light, checking for spots, then set it with the others on the table before grabbing another one.

"That doesn't alter the fact she's a woman."

"With a black belt in self-defense."

"What if she was attacked by a guy with a black belt?" She rested her wrists on the sink, letting her wet soapy hands drip. "It seems to me that in an altercation with opponents who have equal abilities the stronger person wins."

"This is hypothetical, right? Because my mom can take care of herself."

"How do you know?"

"She's packing."

"A gun?"

He nodded. "Besides, you did all the work and I thought you could use a little help cleaning up."

"That's very sweet." Although what she'd really wanted to hear was that he'd stayed just to be with her. That was so sappy, but didn't make it any less true.

"Was this a typical Ryan family gathering?" he asked.

"Usually it's just the four of us. I think Dad was on his best behavior because your mother was here. He probably knew she was packing and figured if he wasn't nice to you she'd shoot him."

"Maybe," he said, chuckling.

He had a nice laugh, Sam thought and laughter chased the tension lines and stress from his face, making him look younger, more carefree. She liked making him laugh.

"What did you do last Thanksgiving?"

Just like that the amusement disappeared. "I was working in the E.R."

"And?"

He started on another glass, rubbing so hard the delicate crystal was in serious jeopardy.

After drying her hands on a towel, she gently took it from him. "What's wrong, Mitch?"

"There wasn't anything to be thankful for that year."

He slapped the towel into his palm, then met her gaze.

"Because your brother died?"

"A few months before," he confirmed. "I knew his addiction was getting worse. When he was doing okay there was no communication. Then he'd get into trouble, either with the cops or he'd wind up in the E.R. That year he was calling all the time." He ran his fingers through his hair, eyes dark and unfocused, brooding. "I tried to get him to go into rehab and he said he would. He always thanked me for taking care of him. But I didn't."

"You couldn't," she amended. "You didn't abandon him, but he was the only one who could help himself." That was something Mitch had to come to terms with. But since she'd opened this can of worms, maybe it would help to dump it all out. "You said that was part of why there was nothing to be thankful for that year. I can't imagine what else—"

"It was a bad time," he said, folding his arms over his chest. "Another time in a whole lot of very bad times."

"Tell me," she urged.

"My wife and I separated the Friday after Thanksgiving."

"After your brother died?" When he nodded, she asked, "What happened?"

"It would be easier to say what didn't happen. I was so wrapped up in taking care of Robbie that I didn't even do routine maintenance on my marriage."

"I don't understand. You weren't being pulled in a different direction at that point. Wasn't there time to reconnect and work on the relationship?"

He shook his head. "It was over."

"But why?"

"She did something that I just couldn't forgive." He met her gaze. "I know what you're thinking. That I'm not taking responsibility for my part in the mess. I freely admit I wasn't there for her. She felt neglected and abandoned. My work came first, then Robbie. I have no doubt that she got tired of coming in a distant third. I'm willing to admit that almost certainly that's what drove her to it."

The woman had cheated on him. She wasn't getting the attention she needed and turned to someone else to meet her needs. It happened all the time. But Sam couldn't understand. Instead of trying to help the man she'd taken a vow to love, she'd made an already overworked, emotionally spent, over-burdened man responsible for her happiness. That level of selfish, self-centered insensitivity was unbelievable to her.

"It's not your fault, Mitch."

His look was wry. "Aren't you the one who always says it takes two to make or break a conflict?"

"Yes. But I wouldn't expect you to follow the three-step plan for conflict resolution when you're seeing a patient whose heart has stopped. When the trauma eases you reprioritize. Your brother was in crisis and you tried to help. That doesn't mean you weren't willing to make changes."

"I appreciate you taking my side, but it's not necessary. It's over. No longer an issue."

That wasn't exactly true. The tug of war in his relationship had left him unable, or unwilling to commit again. He'd become a loner who believed it was every man for himself.

She put her hand on his arm. "I'm sorry I made you think of bad stuff."

"It's okay." He looked down at her. "How about we have some pumpkin pie now?"

Sam's stomach instantly rebelled at the mere mention of food. "Oh, please. I'm too stuffed."

One of Mitch's dark eyebrows rose. "How? You hardly ate a thing."

"What are you? The food police?"

He held up his hands. "Okay. No pie for you."

She blew out a breath. "I didn't mean to snap. I guess it's post-Ryan family meltdown. Sorry."

"It's okay. I'm glad you feel like you can let your guard down with me."

Not so much.

Sam knew her extreme fatigue, aversion to food and a period still missing in action were all symptoms of what happens when you have unprotected sex even just one time. It all added up to the very real probability that she was pregnant. She hadn't done the over-the-counter test yet, but she planned to at the same time she hoped and prayed she was wrong.

She should warn Mitch. Tell him of her suspicions. She might have if he hadn't just shared why the last thing he wanted was more responsibility. Next week she had a doctor's appointment.

If and when she found out she was pregnant, she would tell him. He had a right to know if she was carrying his child. Right now all she had were symptoms and a strong hunch. Without confirmation, she wouldn't say anything and spoil yet another Thanksgiving for him.

Chapter Twelve

Sam was proof that you *could* get pregnant having sex just once without protection. Dr. Rebecca Hamilton had just confirmed what the pregnancy test and her symptoms had been telling her. It was validation that Mitch Tenney had made her want him so badly all she'd been able to think about was the pleasure she'd find in his arms. The memory was still so vivid and the feelings so strong she wondered if they'd ever fade. Probably not.

She would always remember. And if she didn't… She'd have the baby to remind her, which was something because there hadn't been any promises. Mitch wasn't a promise kind of guy.

Sam wasn't sure that finding out she'd be a single mom was a bombshell that should be dropped while her feet were in metal stirrups and her knees in the air. But that's the way it went down.

"All finished." The doctor held out a hand and helped her to a sitting position on the exam table.

"Thanks, Doctor—"

"We're going to be seeing a lot of each other for the next few months. You might as well call me Rebecca."

Rebecca Hamilton was a beautiful brown-eyed blonde who looked too young to be doing what she was doing. Before making the appointment, Sam had done some research and checked out Dr. Hamilton, finding out only good things. Not only that, the office was on Horizon Ridge Parkway in the same building as her own. She'd figured if she were pregnant, she wouldn't have far to go for her prenatal appointments.

Rebecca slipped off her plastic gloves, then toed open the metal trash can and dropped them inside, letting the lid drop shut. "Everything looks good, Samantha—"

"Call me Sam."

"Okay, Sam." The doctor studied her and frowned. "From the look on your face I'm going out on a limb here and take a guess. This pregnancy wasn't planned."

"Not even a little bit."

Rebecca slid her hands into the pockets of her white lab coat. On the breast pocket her name was embroidered in navy letters, along with her specialty—OB/GYN. It was the obstetrics part that had butterflies jumping in Sam's stomach. Now she knew a little person was growing inside her. She definitely had not planned this.

"Why don't you get dressed and meet me in my office? We'll talk," the doctor said.

"Okay."

The answer was automatic and Sam was about to say there wasn't anything to discuss when the door closed. She scooted off the table and slipped on her clothes and low-heeled black shoes. After collecting her coat and purse, she left the room and walked down the hall lined with exam room doors. Rebecca's office was close to the reception area and Sam walked inside, noting all the impressive-looking diplomas on the wall.

The desk held a neat stack of patient charts along with a computer and the typical in/out box. Several metal file cabinets filled one wall.

"Have a seat," Rebecca said, walking in behind her. She sat in the high-backed office chair on the other side of the desk.

Sam noted the two chairs in front and picked the one on the right. "Thanks."

"So, you're going to have a baby." Rebecca smiled.

"I swear it was just once. Without protection," she amended, her cheeks growing warm.

Funny how talking about sex embarrassed her after the intensely personal physical exam she'd just been through. But she felt so incredibly stupid, totally scared.

"I'm not judging you, Sam."

That made one of them. "I guess it comes under the heading 'didn't think it through.'"

"Sometimes that happens. So you regroup and figure things out." Rebecca folded her hands and rested them on the stack of papers in front of her.

"Okay. Right. Figure things out," she repeated like a ventriloquist's dummy.

"Does the father know?"

Sam shook her head. "I wanted to wait until I knew for sure before saying anything to him."

"So he wouldn't be disappointed?" Rebecca suggested.

"That would only happen if he were happy about having a baby."

"Yeah. I was trying to be positive."

"I appreciate that." Sam sighed as she dropped her arm and let her purse slide to the floor beside her. "But, no. He will definitely not be doing the dance of joy when I tell him about this baby."

"Are you sure?"

"Positive."

"How do you feel about having a baby?" Rebecca asked gently.

"That's a good question. I think I'm still in shock. When it wears off you might want to duck."

"Do you want children?"

Sam thought about that for a moment. "Probably. Yeah. Up until now, I haven't given it a lot of consideration what with working on my career goals."

"There are options—"

"No." Sam shook her head. She knew what the doctor was getting at and it was something she wouldn't even consider. She was still in shock, but the life growing inside her suddenly became incredibly real and the need to protect it of paramount importance. "I plan to have this baby."

"Adoption is also a choice."

Let someone else raise her child? She'd been adopted and look how well that turned out. She wasn't completely ungrateful and appreciated that her stepfather hadn't abandoned her. But Mitch had made her face the fact that Arnold Ryan had an agenda that didn't include unselfish motivation. If her mother had lived, things might have been different. Tears burned in her eyes and if it was pregnancy hormones running rampant the months until her baby was born would be very emotional.

But she couldn't help being sad that her mother wasn't here now to confide in about the fact that she was pregnant and alone.

Sam brushed a knuckle beneath her eye as she shook her head. "Let me rephrase and make this very clear. I'm going to have this baby and I will raise it. By myself."

"Okay. But can I give you a piece of advice?" Rebecca asked.

"Of course. You're a healthcare professional and it wouldn't be especially bright not to listen to what you have to say."

"This comes under the personal heading."

Sam nodded. "I see."

"About your baby's father—" Rebecca's gaze slid to a

framed photo on her desk. "Give him a chance to screw up before judging him."

From where she was sitting Sam could see that Rebecca was in the picture with a very good-looking man. Without commenting, she asked, "Who's the guy?"

"Gabriel Thorne. My fiancé."

"He's cute."

"You'll get no argument from me about that." Rebecca actually blushed and sighed.

"He's also a lucky man," Sam said.

"Thanks for saying so. We're really both lucky to have found each other. It wasn't easy. We had a lot to work through." There was a glimmer of radiance shining through the clouds in Rebecca's expression. "Relationships aren't easy. They're messy and complicated. But so worth it when you take a chance."

"That's doctor-speak for I should give him the benefit of the doubt because he might want this baby?"

"I'm saying give him a chance. He just might surprise you."

It had never occurred to Sam not to tell Mitch that he was going to be a father. He'd been through so much and she didn't want to pile on. Still, he had a right to know about his child. But that didn't mean she was looking forward to the conversation. He'd flat-out told her that responsibility wasn't his thing and nothing tied you down, both financially and emotionally, more than a baby.

She studied Rebecca, who suddenly looked older and wiser than when they'd first met in the exam room. She was a woman and a doctor whose specialty was women. She'd probably seen this situation. Sam wasn't the first patient to have an unplanned pregnancy with a man who wasn't eager to commit. Maybe she wasn't being fair to Mitch and assuming the worst. He'd said he wasn't a long-term kind of guy.

But that was before there was a baby. It was possible that when she told him he would be over the moon with happiness about this new life.

She clung to that hope the way a *Titanic* survivor held on to the lifeboat.

There was a knock on Sam's office door which she'd been both anticipating and dreading. "Come in."

Suddenly Mitch was there and her heart started to pound. Normally that was a direct result of her intense reaction to him physically and in every other way. But not today.

She had something to tell him that would change everything and the jury was out on whether or not the change would be in a good way, or a bad one.

He smiled and she felt the power of it down to her toes.

"Hi," he greeted her, lifting his hand in a wave. "I haven't seen you since Thanksgiving."

"I know. I—" What? Missed him? Absolutely. More than she could say. She'd been avoiding him? That, too.

"Mom wanted me to thank you again for inviting her. She had a good time."

"I'm glad. That must mean the two of you are communicating?"

He nodded thoughtfully. "Yeah, we are."

"Good." She was grateful for the small talk and the chance just to look at him, all casual, sexy masculinity. She wanted to enjoy this moment, the easy camaraderie laced with sexual pull.

"The receptionist said you wanted to see me."

Did he need an excuse? This was a hell of a reason. "Yeah. Have a seat." God knew she was glad to be sitting down.

"Okay." He shut the door. Then he moved farther into the

room and rounded her desk, reaching a hand down to pull her to her feet.

"What are you doing?"

"I'm going to kiss you."

He touched his mouth to hers and instantly she started to sizzle. Then he pulled her into his arms and it was a place she wanted to stay forever. The solid warmth and strength of him felt so good. Safe. And safe wasn't a feeling she'd known very much in her life, so she liked it. The need to feel safe was especially powerful since finding out she was going to be a mother. She had to tell him he was going to be a father.

With an effort, she broke the kiss. "Mitch, we can't—"

"I fired you, remember?"

"I know. It's not that. There's something I have to say and when you look at me like that I can't think straight."

His grin grew wider and more smug, more rife with male satisfaction than usual. "I like the sound of that."

"Just so we're clear, that wasn't meant in a good way. Please, listen—"

"Me, first."

He lowered his mouth to hers again and the soft kiss felt too good for words. She automatically opened to him and he took advantage of the invitation. His tongue swept inside and dueled with hers, teasing and caressing until her heart pounded for all the right reasons.

He rubbed his hand up and down her back creating sparks everywhere he touched. Her breasts, more tender and sensitive than she'd ever known, were nestled against his wide chest and the sensation pooled liquid heat in her belly.

His other hand gently squeezed her waist, then slid lower to cup her rear and press her more firmly against his hardness.

He wanted her. If he wanted her enough, there was a chance that it would be okay when she told him…

With an effort, she pulled her mouth from his and struggled to catch her breath. "Oh, boy—"

He was breathing hard, too. "I couldn't have said it better myself."

"Mitch, we have to talk. Really. I'm serious."

"When you say it like that…" He sucked in a breath. "Okay. Shoot."

She stepped away from him and pointed to the chairs in front of her desk. "Go sit over there."

"I like it better over here," he said, brushing his finger over her lips.

"Me, too. But the arrangement isn't especially beneficial to meaningful conversation."

"Talk is cheap and highly overrated."

When he reached for her again, Sam was sorely tempted to let nature take its course. If she wasn't susceptible to his particular brand of charm, the unexpected combination of curtness and caring, she wouldn't be in this predicament in the first place. Two things stopped her from going with it. This was her office and the wrong place for getting personal.

The second was that the next time she was with Mitch, she wanted it to be for all the right reasons, with everything out in the open. She didn't want it to be about putting off telling him what she had to tell him.

She rested her hands firmly on his chest to keep him at bay. "Please sit."

He stared at her for several moments, then backed away and sucked in a breath, letting it out slowly. "What's going on, Sam?"

She stood as tall as possible, straightened her blazer, then said, "I'm pregnant, Mitch."

He didn't exactly recoil, but his body swayed away from her. "This is a joke, right?"

"I'm not kidding."

Finally he sat down. "A baby?"

"Yes," she whispered, slowly lowering herself into her desk chair.

Right off the bat this wasn't going the way her fantasy had. She'd pictured his surprise turning to excitement, elation, unbridled joy. Then he'd pull her against him, lift her off her feet to swing her around, after which he would be properly horrified that he might have hurt her or the baby in his enthusiasm for fatherhood.

It was a cliché; it was stupid. But how she wished that's what he'd done. Considering the dark intensity in his expression, she would settle for shock instead of surprise, which would be an improvement over his current look. It wasn't at all happy. If she had to pick a label, *anger* came pretty close. His silent stare was making her crazy.

"Please say something."

"You're sure?"

"I saw the doctor and she confirmed it."

His eyes hardened as he shook his head. "I can't believe this."

A subtle way of saying she was lying? It felt a lot like an accusation, like a blow to the chest, and seemed to knock the air from her lungs. She shook her head. "I swear, it's the truth."

"This can't be happening—"

"It was just that one time. The first time—" Desire had been all-consuming. Nothing else had mattered except being with him. "We didn't use protection. Obviously you're shocked. I understand."

His mouth thinned. "You couldn't possibly know how I feel."

Sam knew he was thinking about how his ex-wife had betrayed him. At a time in his life when everyone had needed a piece of him she'd cheated and made a mockery of their marriage and left a scar on his heart.

"I didn't do this on purpose," she said. "And I didn't do it all by myself."

His gaze snapped to hers and, if possible, went even darker. "Oh?"

"No." She folded her trembling hands together and put them on her desk. "You were there, too."

"Yeah."

"Were you thinking about protection?" she challenged.

"You'd been in a relationship. I figured you were on birth control."

"*Was* in a relationship. Past tense. That night— With you— There wasn't much discussion about anything," she said miserably. "You're just as responsible for this as I am."

"I remember." He ran his fingers through his hair. "What do you expect from me?"

Cold seemed to roll off him in waves and seeped clear through her, making her shiver. How she wanted the warm safe feeling back. "Excuse me?"

"I'm guessing you've suspected for a while."

"Why do you say that?"

"Thanksgiving. You didn't eat much. No wine. You had symptoms, then, didn't you?"

"Yes, but—"

"And you didn't say anything. What kind of game are you playing?"

"This isn't a game, Mitch. Not to me."

He shifted on the chair and leveled a glare at her. "Then why didn't you tell me sooner?"

"I'd planned to. On Thanksgiving. But you talked about your marriage and the bad stuff—"

"Is this a chick thing? Because that's no excuse."

"I don't know what you're talking about," she protested. "The timing was wrong. We'd had a nice holiday and I didn't want to spoil another one for you. I decided to wait until there was confirmation."

"Now you have it. Is it mine?"

She'd just told him it was his, that she hadn't been on the pill, that he'd been there, too. Which meant he believed she was trying to deceive him. The heat of anger burned through her and it was almost a relief from the cold. "I can't believe you'd ask me that, you arrogant bastard."

"It's a natural question."

"Not for me. I know you went through a lot, but that doesn't give you the right to accuse me of something so ugly. I'm not like your ex. I don't lie. I'm carrying your child and I thought you had a right to know. My mistake."

He stood and looked down at her. "So, I repeat. What do you expect from me?"

"Not a damn thing." She stood, too, and met his gaze without wavering. "I said what I had to. Now get out of my office."

Without another word he left.

Sam sank into her chair, shaking so badly that her legs wouldn't hold her up. This wasn't good for the baby, but she couldn't seem to stop. Some conflict coach she was. There were a dozen different ways she could have handled that situation. But as much as she believed in using the right words, the reality was nothing she'd said would have helped because she was incapable of being rational.

Against the odds and her better judgment, she'd fallen in love with Mitch Tenney. Under those circumstances, it was impossible to be logical.

Chapter Thirteen

The E.R. was too quiet.

Mitch lounged at the nurses' station feeling restless and uneasy. He much preferred being too busy because now he had time on his hands. Too much time to think about how he'd treated Sam when she'd told him she was pregnant. If he could have been a bigger ass, he wasn't sure how.

It had been a week since that day in her office, when she'd dropped the baby bomb. If she hadn't waited so long to give him the news, things might have gone better, but probably not. As if that wasn't bad enough, he'd implied she was trying to pass off another guy's baby as his.

The whole scene was like a train wreck that played in slow motion, over and over in his mind. He'd been deliberately acting like the arrogant ass she accused him of being before ordering him out of her office. He'd wanted out of there, but it was the last relieved breath he'd drawn in seven days.

He'd called her but she wouldn't talk to him. And why should she?

Mitch had felt rage and betrayal when his wife had told him the whole truth about what she'd done to their baby. But now he hated what happened even more because the unimaginable manipulation was responsible for his knee-jerk reaction and unjustified attack on Sam. She didn't deserve that.

He realized the computer keys behind him were quiet and Rhonda, the E.R. nurse/manager, was staring at him.

"What?" he said.

She folded her arms over her ample breasts. "You look terrible."

"Thank you."

"It wasn't a compliment," she shot back. "And your attitude lately stinks."

"If it wasn't politically incorrect, I'd say bite me."

"See, that's what I mean." Her brown eyes narrowed on him. "You were making progress in that area, but recently there's been a noticeable relapse. The mumbling to yourself is new."

"And your point is?"

"What's going on with you, Mitch?"

Before he could tap-dance around the question, she looked down and reached for the pager at her waist. She met his gaze. "The paramedics called a few minutes ago. They just arrived with a pregnant woman. I'll go check it out."

He nodded. "Let me know when I'm up."

She disappeared down the hall and Mitch missed her acid tongue because he was all alone with his thoughts again. He sat down at the computer, but before he could go online, he heard someone behind him.

When he saw Rhonda, he said, "That was quick. False alarm?"

"It's Sam," she said.

"What? With the paramedics?"

She nodded. "She's bleeding and—"

He didn't wait for more, but took off at a run and found her in trauma bay two. Half-sitting up in the bed, she had an IV going and looked pale, scared.

"Sam? What's wrong?"

The question was automatic and not the least bit professional. He didn't feel like a doctor; he was a guy concerned about a girl. After looking at her paperwork for pulse, respiration and blood pressure, the numbers danced in front of his eyes without sticking in his brain. The last notation was that the patient's physician would meet her at Mercy Medical.

"Mitch, I didn't mean to come here—" She ran her tongue over her lips. "I started spotting. I called Dr. Hamilton—"

"Why didn't you call *me?*"

Her eyes widened then were filled with hurt. "You're not my doctor."

"You're pregnant with my child. You should have called me so I could—" He stopped. What could he do? Panic more than he was already?

He saw trauma patients all the time but he'd never lost it like he had just now. Sam wasn't just another patient. She was Sam. And she was pregnant with his child.

On the white cotton blanket covering her from the waist down, Sam's fingers curled into a fist. "I called *my* doctor, Mitch. Transport by ambulance was her way of being overly cautious. I tried to talk her into another E.R., but this is the closest—for her and me. She'll be here soon, so don't concern yourself with me."

Don't concern himself? That advice was way too late. He was already concerned for her. "Did you fall?" When she shook her head, he asked, "Any cramping?"

"The bleeding just started. It's not that much, but I got scared—"

The door opened and Rebecca Hamilton walked in. Mitch had seen her in the E.R. before. She nodded at him. "Hi, Mitch."

"Rebecca." He ran his fingers through his hair.

"Hi, Sam. How are you feeling?"

Sam let out a relieved breath. "Hanging in there. The ambulance was great fun. There's nothing I like more than being the center of attention. It's even better when burly men carry you around."

"Sass and sarcasm. Both positive signs." Rebecca smiled. "The ambulance comes under the heading of better safe than sorry since you were planning to drive yourself to the E.R.—"

"What?" Mitch couldn't believe he'd heard right. Why hadn't she called him. "You're bleeding and you were going to drive yourself?"

Rebecca looked at him. "I can take it from here, Mitch."

That was a subtle way of saying get the heck out. He shook his head. "Sam is my— We're—" He looked at Sam, but she showed no sign that she intended to bail him out. "It's my baby."

"Good to know." Rebecca nodded, but her doctor face never budged. "If you'll step outside, I'd like to take a look at my patient now."

"Sam, let me—"

She shook her head. "I'd like to handle this privately, with my doctor."

Both women stared at him and he finally walked out, but he paced the hall and wore a new path in the floor outside her door. It was killing him not to know what was going on in that room. A little knowledge was a dangerous thing. Pregnant women could have complications. What if something happened to Sam? Or the baby? God, he hated not being in control, not calling the shots. What if—

Before he could finish that thought, the door opened and Rebecca stood there. "Come on in, Mitch."

He moved close to the bed and started to reach for Sam,

but she curled her fingers into a fist again. He looked at Rebecca. "Is she all right, Doc?"

"The bleeding has stopped. That's a good sign."

"And?"

"Sam's blood pressure is normal."

"So what's going on with the baby? What caused the episode?"

"Sometimes early in a pregnancy it just happens. That doesn't necessarily mean there's anything wrong."

"That's good." He glanced at her but she wouldn't look at him. "So what now?"

"Sam knows what to do."

"I'd like to know, too."

"Since when, Mitch?" Sam asked, her voice all sharp edges.

"She needs to take it easy," Rebecca interjected. "Stay off her feet. Take care of herself and her baby. No stress."

"Done," he said.

"Wait a second." Sam glared at him. "This isn't your call to make."

"Watch me," he said. "You're not lifting a finger until the doc says it's okay."

"So now you're convinced it's your baby?" Sam asked.

He winced. She had a finely tuned sarcastic streak going, and it was aimed directly at him. Although he couldn't blame her. "I screwed up."

"No?" She gasped, but it was exaggerated and mocking. "The mighty Mitch Tenney made a mistake and is actually admitting it? The world has gone mad."

"Sam, take it easy—"

"The key here," Rebecca said, "is rest and relaxation. Whatever tension is between you two needs to go on a back burner for now."

"Excellent advice, Doctor," Mitch said. "I will see to it that Sam gets all the R and R she can stand."

"Good." Rebecca smiled as if he'd just passed some kind of test, then reached for the pager hooked on the waistband of her pink scrubs. "Gotta go. I have a patient upstairs in labor and she's ready to have her baby."

"I'm glad you didn't make a special trip here for me," Sam said.

Mitch was pretty glad she'd been there, too, because he wouldn't have been much good. "Thanks, Rebecca."

"Don't hesitate to call if you need anything." She waved on her way out the door.

"So," Mitch said, "I'll see about getting you signed out then I'll take you home."

"Don't bother. I'll call someone—"

"No, you won't."

"First of all you're working. You can't just leave."

"It's a slow night. If it doesn't stay that way, one of the other guys in the group can cover the rest of my shift."

The look she gave him was meant to intimidate but made her look more like a lost kitten. "I meant it when I said I don't want anything. Let's just agree to disagree and move forward. Separately. That's best for both of us—"

The door opened and Arnold Ryan stood there. Great, Mitch thought. It should have made him feel better that a bigger jerk than himself had just arrived. Funny how he just knew the situation was headed even further south.

"Samantha? What's going on?" Ryan demanded.

"Dad." Sam pushed herself up a little higher in the bed. "What are you doing here?"

"I was in my office and got a call that you were in the E.R. Are you all right?"

"Yes."

He looked at Mitch. "Tell me the feeling I have that you're somehow involved is completely wrong."

"Dad, it's not what you think. I—"

"Don't tell me what I think," he snapped.

So much for rest and relaxation, Mitch thought. "Look, Mr. Ryan, she needs to take it easy. Just give her a break—"

"Stay out of this, Doctor. It's between me and my daughter."

And me, he thought. "I'm not going to stand here and watch you bully her. Give her a break or—"

"Stop," Sam said. She looked up at him. "I'll handle this."

"You need to rest," he reminded her.

"Will someone kindly tell me what's going on?" Ryan demanded.

Sam looked at her father. "I'm here because I'm bleeding, Dad."

He frowned. "Was there an accident? Samantha, you drive too fast. I've always told you to slow down—"

"There was no accident," Mitch said, reading the irony of those words in Sam's eyes.

"I'm going to have a baby," she said bluntly. "I was spotting, but the doctor was just here and says there's no reason to think there's a problem with the pregnancy. I just have to take it easy. And before you ask, Mitch is the father."

It was the first time Mitch had ever seen Arnold Ryan shocked into silence. If only it would last.

Anger burned bright in the other man's eyes. "Samantha, I'm extraordinarily disappointed in you. I brought you up better than this."

As a doctor Mitch had taken an oath to do no harm and he'd never wanted to break that vow more than he did now. "You're disappointed because she's pregnant? Or because she was with me?" he asked. "If Jax the jerk was the father would that make it okay?"

"He'd do the right thing by Samantha and marry her," Ryan said, disapproval flashing in his eyes. "What are your intentions toward my daughter?"

"I don't think that's any of your business—"

Ryan took a step forward. "I'm making it my concern."

"I would never hurt Sam."

"You don't think getting her pregnant is hurting her—"

"Dad, please…"

He ignored her. "Don't make the mistake of thinking that this…personal involvement with my daughter will bullet-proof your career, Dr. Tenney. You're still on probation and one false move—"

"Dad, this isn't the time."

Ignoring her, Ryan continued his tirade. "If you so much as look at anyone the wrong way, you're gone, Doctor. Samantha is having a difficult enough time getting her life on track. Thanks to you, now she has to deal with this. I really don't—"

"Dad—" The sharpness of her voice got his attention and she took a deep breath. "I've had enough of you belittling me and my job. It stops right now."

He looked genuinely shocked. "Samantha, you've never spoken to me that way before."

"Then it's past time I did." She met his gaze. "I need you to stop giving me orders. You can't tell me who to marry or what to do. I'm a grown woman. I'm going to be a mother. I'll be responsible for my child. You're going to be a grand-father and I want you to be a part of my life, but not if you tell me how to run it."

Go, Sam, Mitch thought. For the life of him he couldn't wipe off the smug, almost satisfied grin he knew was on his face.

"Samantha, what are you saying?"

Her expression was firm and clearly indicated she would tolerate no argument. "If you can't say nice things, and only nice things, I want you to leave. And I don't want to see you until you can."

"You don't mean that."

"On the contrary, I've never meant anything more."

Ryan shot an angry parting look at her. Without further acknowledgment of Mitch, he turned and left the room.

Mitch wanted to pump his arm and holler "Way to go." He couldn't be more proud of Sam, but then he saw the tears sliding down her cheeks.

"Don't cry, Sam."

He sat on the side of the bed and pulled her into his arms. She was a hell of a roller-coaster ride. First she'd scared the crap out of him. Then she'd told her pompous, arrogant father where to get off.

And now she was crying. He couldn't stand it when she cried. And it was his fault. If not for him, her relationship with her family wouldn't be in jeopardy. If not for him, she wouldn't be pregnant and there'd have been no reason for the scene she'd just been through. She sniffled and her shoulders shook from the effort to pull herself together.

He hated that he was responsible for upsetting her. Almost as much as he'd hated seeing her in a hospital bed, a trauma that had reduced him from respected doctor to a mere mortal man scared for the woman he cared too much about.

He hated it because it was a symptom that he was in deep trouble.

Sam was so confused.

In her apartment, sitting with her feet up on her chenille

corner group, she watched Mitch banging pots and pans in the kitchen and wondered how this had happened. One minute she'd been lying in a hospital bed in his arms trying to make herself push him away. Not an hour later he'd insisted on carrying her upstairs to her place. He was one burly medic she didn't mind having haul her around.

That pesky romantic streak had made her putty in his hands. How ironic was that? She'd taken two independent steps forward with the ultimatum to her father and so many back that she couldn't even *see* independence from where she was sitting.

She'd tried to tell Mitch to go away but couldn't be sorry he'd ignored her.

"Dinner is just about ready."

He leaned a broad shoulder against the wall just outside the kitchen and folded his arms over his chest. In jeans and a T-shirt he looked more delicious than any food he was whipping up. The fact that she still thought so even after the way he'd acted about the pregnancy put her pretty high up on the pathetic scale.

"I'm not very hungry," she said.

"You need something. You're eating for two." He went back in the kitchen, making further argument a challenge.

If only he'd reacted this way when she'd told him about the baby. She glanced at the expanse of beige carpet on the other side of her coffee table and thought about the night that passion for Mitch had made her go up in flames and resulted in the new life inside her. She'd been conflicted about this child until the possibility of losing it became very real. A powerful feeling of protectiveness came over her and she knew she'd lie, cheat, beg or steal to take care of this baby.

Mitch brought a tray with a bowl of split pea soup and a

ham sandwich from the kitchen and set it on her lap. The smell of the soup she normally loved turned her stomach.

She sucked in a breath and pointed to the plate. "Take it away. If you have any compassion or consideration for my dignity, you'll remove that stat."

"It's good for you—"

"I don't care. I'm telling you the baby doesn't like it and if it's not gone in ten seconds you'll be sorry." She put her hand over her mouth.

"Okay." He took it out of her sight, then came back and sat on the coffee table beside her. "Tell me what sounds good."

"Peanut butter."

"Coming right up."

He disappeared and returned a few minutes later with a sandwich.

"Thank you." It actually tasted good and made her realize she was hungry. After eating most of it, she said, "I don't mean to be a diva, but there are some smells that just set off the nausea."

"It's not like I've never seen anyone get sick," he pointed out.

True. But it wasn't high on her list of things to do in front of him. "Still, I'd rather avoid the experience if at all possible."

"I understand." He took the tray back in the kitchen, then returned with a cup of tea and handed it to her.

"Let's get one thing straight. You don't have a clue." She vigorously dunked the tea bag in the mug of hot water. "You have no idea how it feels to be pregnant. You can't possibly understand what it feels like to be accused of…well, the things you implied. And that begs the question. If you believe I'm capable of such despicable behavior, why are you here being nice to me?"

"Because it's my baby."

She wasn't sure what had changed for him, but the disappointment trickling through her was very identifiable. His presence here had nothing to do with any feelings for her and she so wanted it to be about that.

"I see."

"No, you don't." He let out a long breath. "But I owe you an explanation."

"That's all right. I get it. You've been great, but I'm fine now. You should go—"

"I'll go if that's what you want, but not before you agree to hear me out."

They stared at each other for several moments and the expression in his eyes told her whatever he had to say was going to be bad. Suddenly she was afraid. She didn't want to know, but knew she had to.

"All right."

He nodded and held her gaze for a couple of seconds before saying, "My wife was pregnant."

Of all the things it was possible for him to reveal that was the last thing she'd expected. "With your baby?" she blurted out.

"Yeah."

"It's just that I thought— When you talked about her— I just had the impression that she'd cheated on you—" And when she'd told him she was pregnant he'd felt the need to ask if it was his.

"She cheated, but not the way you mean."

"I don't understand."

"You already know about my brother and how I tried to help him."

She nodded. "And that she felt neglected. I thought you were saying that she'd turned to another man for attention."

"I could have understood that."

His eyes turned icy, desolate, and Sam gripped the mug until her knuckles turned white, grateful for the warmth. If only it could reach inside where she was the coldest. What could be worse than the woman you trusted cheating with another man?

As much as she didn't want to know, the silence was unbearable. "What did she do?"

"Without discussing the idea with me she suspended all birth control and got pregnant. She came up with some song and dance about forgetting to take the Pill."

"She got pregnant on purpose." It wasn't a question. She was almost afraid to ask. But like an accident on the side of the road, she couldn't look away from this now. "What happened to the baby?"

"She said she miscarried. It wasn't until after our divorce that she confessed what she'd done."

"What?"

He met her gaze and the truth was there in the dark intensity of his eyes. "She got rid of it."

Sam was shocked. She sat up straight and swung her legs over the side of the sofa. After setting her mug down, she whispered, "How could she do that to you?"

"To me?" His laugh was bitter. "She said it was all my fault. I was too preoccupied trying to save the world to pay any attention to her and she didn't want to raise a child by herself."

"Oh, Mitch—" So it was a trust issue after all, just not as simple as she'd believed. He'd been deceived in the most elemental and hurtful way. She reached out and put her hand on his arm. "I'm so sorry."

"No, I'm sorry."

"Don't be."

"I am. It had nothing to do with you, but the bad stuff was

all right there, as if no time had passed. The feeling of being invisible, irrelevant, used. She stole something from me—not once but twice." The anger was back in his voice when he said, "That day you told me about being pregnant… The news came out of left field. Again. It wasn't my finest hour. I was wrong to take it out on you."

"Maybe. But your reaction makes sense now."

It made so much sense. The truth of the situation made her sick to her stomach all over again. She and the baby were a responsibility he in no way wanted. The fact that he was being sweet and solicitous only heightened her sadness and pain by giving her a glimpse of what might have been.

Mitch would never believe she hadn't gotten pregnant in order to trap him. Without trust, love wasn't possible.

"I'm so sorry all that happened to you." That was an understatement, Sam thought. They might have had a chance if things had been different.

"It's in the past. I don't mean to whine."

"It never crossed my mind that you were."

He shrugged. "Just thought you should know."

Was it better or worse now that she did? His anger wasn't directed at her, but there was no way he'd ever care, and risk hurt and deception. And suddenly she just wanted to be alone. She was tired. The fear she was going to lose the baby had drained her and she wasn't sure how long she could hold herself together. She'd cried in his arms twice when things with her father had gone badly. Who was going to hold her when she cried over Mitch?

"I'd like you to go," she said.

He looked up, surprised. "What?"

"I'm worn out. It's been a long day."

"You go to bed, I'll just hang here in case you need anything."

"That's not necessary. I'm fine." That was a lie, but what else could she say? "Rest is what I need. Doctor's orders."

"I don't want to leave you alone."

He was going to force her to say the words. She needed a clean break because it hurt too much to have him there knowing she could never have *him*.

"Alone is better than being an obligation."

"That's not why I'm here," he protested.

"I appreciate the lie, but we both know that's all it is. What you went through was awful. And if I could change that I'd do it in a heartbeat. But the reality is that the past ate up too much of you and there's nothing left over for me."

"I want to take care of you."

"And I want your love. I understand why it can't happen, but I won't settle for less." Her throat felt tight and it was difficult to say the words. "So it's better if you just go now."

"Sam, you don't mean it—"

"I do. Please, leave, Mitch."

He stared at her for several long moments, his eyes going darker and more intense. "Are you sure about this?"

"Very." She put more conviction into that one word than she would have thought possible. But, thanks to him, she was the new and improved Sam. She knew what she wanted and wasn't afraid to say so. Let the chips fall where they may.

Finally he nodded, and stood. "You'll call if you need me?"

What she needed and always would from him he couldn't give her. "If there's anything you need to know, I'll get in touch," she promised.

He leaned down and she knew he was going to kiss her. She turned her face and his lips brushed her cheek.

"I don't want to see you in my E.R. again."

"Yes, sir." She would never know how she managed to smile.

When the door closed behind him Sam felt more alone than she'd ever felt in her life. Her father would probably never speak to her again but she hadn't been able to stand by and say nothing while he was putting down the man she loved. Her lashing out could very well cost her the only family she had.

Worse, she'd lost the love of her life, and the pain of that realization sliced clear to her soul.

Chapter Fourteen

"Are you all right, Mitch?"

He straightened the silverware on the white tablecloth. "Of course. Why do you ask?"

Ellen Tenney's expression was wry as she looked across their table in Primo's, a steak house at the Suncoast Hotel in Summerlin. "We haven't exactly been close for a long time. Taking me to dinner is out of character."

"Is it too much to ask that you could stop being a detective for a couple of hours and just relax?"

"It's okay to ask, but I can't promise anything. I look at patterns. I notice things. I ask questions." She glanced around the elegant, second-floor dining room with floor-to-ceiling windows looking out on the lights stretching across the Vegas Valley. "And dinner here is a major red flag."

"I can't take my mom out for a nice meal?"

"I'm not complaining. But there are hundreds of places that would be nice. Primo's is *nice,* if you know what I mean. That makes me ask questions. Like what's going on with you?" She shrugged. "So sue me."

In some weird way the fact his mother could still read him was cool. He felt like a drowning man going down for the third time. A week ago he'd left Sam after bringing her home from the E.R. He'd thought about calling her and every time he'd picked up the phone, he remembered the death of hope in her eyes. Warm optimism disappeared and he felt as if he'd stomped the stuffing out of Tinkerbell. He'd wanted her to understand why he'd acted like a jerk and now she did but it didn't help much. Telling her hadn't changed his past or the man he'd turned into because of it. He still tended to find trusting anyone a challenge.

Yet he hadn't wanted to leave her. Walking out that door had felt like cutting his heart out with a spoon. The only reason he'd gone was the fear of stressing her out after what she'd already been through. He would never do anything to hurt Sam or his child.

Seven days had gone by. He could feel her slipping away from him and didn't know how to stop it. He'd spent so much of his life watching out for Robbie and patching people up but he didn't know how to fix himself.

"What is it, Mitch? You look like you lost your best friend."

That wasn't surprising since he'd lost Sam and she was his best friend.

Before he could answer, the waiter in white shirt and black vest arrived to take their orders. Throwing her cholesterol levels to the wind, Ellen ordered a filet mignon and he got the lamb, then selected a good bottle of wine. After the bread basket arrived, there was an awkward silence while his mother put her cop face back on and let the lack of conversation drag on to make him feel obligated to fill it.

So he did. Through their dinner he made small talk about his career, the weather, upcoming holidays. Anything and everything that wasn't of a personal nature.

After the waiter cleared their plates and they decided to split a huge piece of chocolate cake, she gave him the narrow-eyed detective look again. "So are you ready to talk yet?"

"I thought that's what I've been doing."

She shook her head. "You threw me a bone, but it's not what I'm really after."

"And what would that be?"

"I want to know why we're here. What's this dinner all about?" She pointed her finger at him. "And I want the truth."

He twirled the stem of his water glass. "There's just something unnatural about a guy's mom being a detective. This isn't casual conversation, it's witness interrogation."

Instead of being intimidated, she grinned. "If you are what you eat, that lamb should have made you more accommodating."

"Baa."

"Better," she said, then laughed. Their dessert arrived with two forks and she took a taste. "That is too good for words."

"Good enough to stop twenty questions?"

"Not even for money." Her expression turned serious. "Don't get me wrong. This evening means more to me than you'll probably ever know. And maybe I'm going about it all wrong. But I'm your mother and I know that something's bothering you. If you want to talk, I'm happy to listen."

That was when he felt the weight of everything he'd carried for so long. Robbie had been his brother and the burden was heavy. But not as much as the failure he'd lived with since losing him.

"I'm sorry I let you down. I'm sorry I couldn't save Robbie."

Ellen looked like he whipped out a gun and aimed. "This is about Robbie?"

"Partly," he admitted. "The thing is, it was my responsibility to take care of him. In school I included him with my friends. I made sure he didn't flunk out. If anyone picked on him they had to deal with me. And then I went to college and medical school."

"You're entitled to a life," Ellen said.

"But he changed."

Her mouth thinned. "Robbie got in with a bad crowd."

"I should have stayed," Mitch said.

"No. After your father was shot, all you ever wanted was to be a doctor. It would have been wrong to put your life on hold for your brother. He needed to find his own way."

"But he didn't. That's why I came back to Las Vegas for my residency. He needed me. And I tried to help him. I dropped everything if he called. I was there for him. I tried to get him into rehab—"

"You think it's your fault, Mitch?"

"It is, Mom." He met her gaze. "I finally told him he was on his own. My marriage was failing because I put it last. I had to try and salvage it."

"You were right to try," she said. "But, for what it's worth, I'm glad you're not with her. She was a manipulative, conniving, cunning schemer."

He smiled at the fiercely maternal look on her face. "Don't sugarcoat it, Mom. Tell me how you really feel."

"I didn't like her. Ever. And I'm not sorry she's no longer in you life."

Funny, Detective Tenney was right on the money about his ex and she didn't even know the whole story. There was no point in bringing it up now, but it didn't seem so much like a failure after hearing her opinion.

"Anyway, the night he overdosed, Robbie called me." He stared out the window, not wanting to see the censure in her eyes. "I didn't take the call. And I just wanted to tell you I'm sorry that I let you down."

"I can't believe you blame yourself for what happened to Robbie." She sounded surprised.

Mitch looked at her then. "After Dad was killed, you always told me to watch out for my brother. That I was the responsible one. But I wasn't. Not the last time."

"Oh, Mitch." She looked down and shook her head. "I'm the one who should apologize."

"What for?"

"For making you feel as if you had to be a substitute father to your brother. I'm so sorry for anything I said or did to make you think he was your job. If anyone was to blame, it was me. With your father gone, I was the sole support of the family. I had to work and that meant there just wasn't enough time to spend with my boys." Tears welled in her eyes and she didn't look like a tough detective anymore. She looked like a mom, sad for the child she'd lost. "Robbie's weakness wasn't your fault, son. He's the only one who could have helped himself and for whatever reason he didn't. Or couldn't."

"You really believe that?"

She nodded. "And after he died, there was a distance between you and me. It felt like I'd lost both my boys and I didn't understand. Funny, I can get information from a suspect, but not from my own son."

More weight lifted from his shoulders and he smiled. "Food for thought."

"No kidding."

"We'll have to do this more often," he said.

"Are you buying?"

"Yeah."

"Count me in." She sipped from her water glass, then met his gaze. "Speaking of food, I had a good time at Sam's on Thanksgiving. How is she?"

Just like that it was Interrogation Central again. For some reason he didn't mind. "She's okay."

"Care to elaborate?"

It seemed to be the night for confessions and they said it was good for the soul. "She's pregnant, Mom. It's my baby."

Ellen's eyes went wide, then the news sank in and she smiled. "I'm going to be a grandmother?"

"Yes." He braced himself for questions about his intentions. If they were getting married.

"That's wonderful, Mitch. Sam's a nice girl. I like her very much."

"How does she rate on your detective radar? Conniving, cunning, deceitful or scheming?"

"None of the above. She's a keeper and I just have to ask what she sees in you."

"Thanks, Mom. I just got a warm fuzzy."

He teased back, but her words struck a chord. What *did* Sam see in him?

From the very first she'd worked her tail off to salvage him because she felt he had something to offer. Of course it was her job. He knew that. But she went above and beyond the call of duty. He'd been crabby, grumpy and ungrateful. She'd been sunny, caring and brimming with optimism. Yet he'd managed to crush that out of her.

She'd told him he had too much baggage and there was nothing left over for her. The last thing he wanted was to make another mistake. His spirit was lighter, knowing his mother didn't blame him for Robbie's death. But he couldn't stand it if he did anything to crush the light out of Sam any more than he already had.

Except it wasn't that simple.

He'd missed her like crazy. She was all he could think about and being with her was the only time in his life that he could remember being truly and completely happy.

Talking to his mother made him remember what Robbie had gone through. He'd had a weakness for crystal meth and cocaine and couldn't shake it. Drugs were an addiction. Until Sam Mitch hadn't really understood what it felt like to crave something you couldn't get out of your system. He hadn't been able to relate to the feeling of wanting something with every fiber of his being.

That's the way he wanted Sam.

But she wanted love and a happy ending and his track record in that department was in the dumper. Her father was right about him. He was the wrong man and would only make her unhappy. So he was trying to do what was right for her.

It would be easier to be noble if he didn't love her so much.

What did an unmarried, pregnant-and-fighting-nausea woman do on a Saturday night in Las Vegas?

If that woman was Sam, she would stay home and try to keep a stiff upper lip at the same time her life looked like a train wreck. She had to snap out of it because there were plans to make, another life to think about that was more important than being rejected by the man she'd fallen for. Getting over him wouldn't be easy, but she'd do it. Or at least pretend.

Mitch hadn't called and that hurt. She couldn't pretend it didn't. Her father wasn't speaking to her. She'd hoped to hear from Connor and Fiona. The fact she hadn't hurt, too.

Good grief, she was pathetic. Enough, already. It was time to snap out of it. No one liked a whiner.

There was a knock on the door and Sam's heart took a flying leap. Mitch!

As she rose from the couch, her hand automatically went to her hair, which was falling out of the scrunchy on top of her head. There'd been no reason to put on makeup and she looked like something the cat yakked up. A phone call would have been nice, but who was she to complain?

After rounding the coffee table, she forced herself to slowly walk to the door. When she turned the dead bolt, she noticed her hand was shaking. That was nothing compared to what her insides were doing.

She opened the door and did a double take because she'd been expecting someone else. "Connor."

He slid his hands into the pockets of his khakis. "Hi, Sam."

"I wasn't expecting you."

"Probably I should have called, but—" He looked around her. "Do you have company?"

"No. I'm alone." That sounded so pathetic. She was going to have to work on it harder.

"Can I come in?"

"Oh. Sure." She stepped back and opened the door wider. "Sorry."

"That's my line."

After turning the dead bolt, she looked at him. "What?"

"I'm sorry."

"For?"

"Not being here for you." He shoved his hand through his hair. "Dad just told me you're pregnant."

It never occurred to Sam that her father would keep the news to himself. By this time she figured Connor and Fiona knew and were simply avoiding her.

"Wow, I—"

"Why didn't you tell me?" In his eyes, anger mixed with something that looked a lot like hurt.

"I figured news would spread. I'm still getting used to the idea. I didn't think—"

"Damn right you didn't," he said heatedly. "The least you could do is let me know I'm going to be an uncle."

"But I'm not really your sister." She did her best to keep any hint of a whine from her tone.

"Says who?"

"Well, no one did in so many words. It's just I don't expect you to feel any obligation to me just because your father put a roof over my head. I was adopted."

"Yeah. I got the memo. Even if I didn't, *you* never forget about it."

"It's a fact."

He nodded. "It's also a fact that I love you. You're my sister just as much as Fiona. You're family, Sam. That means you don't keep stuff like a baby to yourself."

"Your father did."

"I'm not my father." His eyes went dark. "I'm your big brother and that's not going to change. Ever. Got it? I've only ever treated you like a sister. You're the one who can't get past the lack of a biological connection which is not a big deal to the rest of us. Including Dad, by the way. He's just as hard on me and Fee in case you haven't noticed."

"Are you saying it's my problem?"

"Yeah," he said, nodding. "If you're willing to throw away a perfectly good brother then that's up to you, but I wouldn't recommend it."

That's when she burst into tears.

The next thing she knew, Connor had pulled her into his arms. "Don't cry, Sam."

"I c-can't help it. Hormones have taken over my body. And—" she struggled to control the sobs "—you're too s-sweet for words."

"Yeah. Be sure and spread the word to all your friends. The

single ones. I like tall, but someone your height isn't a deal breaker. Blonde, brunette. Redhead. I'm not fussy."

She couldn't help laughing. "You're bad."

"You just said I was sweet," he reminded her.

"That was before you were hitting on all my friends."

He rubbed his chin on the top of her head. "I'm not coming on to them. It's better if you do the work."

She stepped back and punched him playfully in the arm. "I'm not doing your dirty work for you. That's not what sisters are for. I'd be happy to introduce my brother to someone smart, funny and reasonably attractive that I think would be good for him."

"So I'm your brother now?"

She took his hand and led him over to the corner group, pulling him down beside her. "You've always been. I guess I've been afraid to let my guard down, afraid of losing anyone else I care about."

"Like your mom." He took her hand between both of his. "That was a tough break. But now you're going to be a mother. Would you want this child to hold back and let life pass by without really living it?"

"Of course not."

"Okay, then."

She tipped her head to the side and studied him. "I bet you're a really good attorney."

"I am." He grinned. "And speaking of that, Fiona said to tell you she would be here with me, but she's got a client dinner. She'll be over tomorrow."

"I'll look forward to that."

"So I'm going to be an uncle?"

"Of course this baby is all about you." She laughed, then turned serious.

"Of course." His expression was protective as he scanned her face. "Are you really okay? Dad said you were in the E.R."

"I'm fine. There was some spotting, but it stopped right away. The doctor says it happens sometimes and isn't a cause for alarm. So I'm going to be a mom."

He shook his head. "Just so you know, I plan to spoil my niece or nephew until he or she is the most obnoxious child on the planet."

Tears welled in her eyes again. "I'm glad there will be a strong, kind man in his life."

"What about Mitch?"

The name was like a knife to her heart. "You know?"

"Dad didn't hold back."

Why should he start now?

"I have no reason to believe that Mitch intends to be a part of this child's life," she explained, proud of herself for keeping her voice from breaking. The slight lip tremble was tougher to control.

Connor's mouth tightened. "You have legal recourse, Sam. He needs to take some responsibility—"

"That's the last thing I want to do," she interrupted. "I don't want to force anything on him."

"This is his child, too. That should count for something."

It should. But she didn't want her baby to ever feel like she did, like a nuisance someone got stuck with. As sweet as Connor was being, he'd never understand what it felt like to lose your whole world and have no alternative but to fit into someone else's—someone who didn't welcome you with open arms.

"Let's be clear about something," she said. "This is my child. I've informed Mitch that he's going to be a father and the rest is up to him."

"But, Sam—"

"No buts." She shook her head. "I don't want to be a duty to him. I don't want the baby to be nothing more than a duty, either. I don't want anything if it's just about appearances."

"Do you think he's that type?"

"I don't know what to think because he hasn't said anything."

"What do you mean?"

"I haven't heard from him since he brought me home from the E.R." And acted as if he cared.

Lack of contact spoke volumes about how he really felt. He hadn't asked for this pregnancy to happen, but neither had she. And now bringing a new life into the world was the most important thing. His actions would suggest he didn't agree. Now she knew what he'd been through had shattered his capacity for caring. She had the rest of her life to come to terms with it.

"He's probably been busy," Connor suggested.

"Don't," she said, holding up her hand. "I refuse to get my hopes up. The reality is that he can't be there for me."

"Then he's a complete idiot."

"I love you for that, big brother." She smiled sadly. "But it's best if I start getting over him."

A stubborn, angry, determined look slid into Connor's narrowed eyes. "Don't write him off just yet, Sam."

"Give me one good reason why not."

"Because you're in love with him," Connor said with conviction. When she started to protest, he held up a hand. "I'm not asking for independent clarification or denial. I have an instinct for these things."

She didn't think anything could surprise or amuse her under the circumstances, but her brother did both. "You have an instinct for love?"

"I do. In some circles I'm known as Counselor Cupid."

She laughed. "Now you're pulling my leg."

"Yes. But in your case, I have a strong feeling that I'm right and you could use some counsel."

"I don't like that look."

"What look?"

"That look," she said, pointing. "Tell me what you're thinking."

"Besides beating him up?"

"You wouldn't."

"Don't be too sure."

"Please, promise me that you won't make things worse by confronting Mitch," she said.

"I'd never make your life more complicated." He made a cross over his heart, then held up two fingers. "Scout's honor."

She nodded, but the reality was that things couldn't really get any worse. Committed men didn't go silent. The sound of silence told her that she was in love with a man who couldn't love her back.

It was time to face the fact that she needed to make plans for her and the baby. Alone.

Chapter Fifteen

"There's someone here to see you."

At the sound of the voice, Mitch looked up from the medical journal he was reading. Rhonda was standing in the doorway of the break room.

"Who?"

The nurse lifted one shoulder in a shrug. "Maybe CIA. Could be Homeland Security."

If he wasn't in such a crappy mood he might have cracked a smile at that. "Did he show you cop creds?"

"No. But he's wearing a suit. Looks like the official type."

"And just what does that look like?"

"Rugged. Hunky. In a civilized, smart sort of way."

"You watch too much TV."

"Maybe." She shrugged again. "Everything but the medical shows. That leaves mostly crime scene stuff."

"Did you ask his name?"

"I may be hooked on homicides, but I'm not stupid. He wouldn't say who he is, but was quite clear that he's not leaving until you give him five minutes."

"Okay, then. Bring him back."

When she was gone, Mitch refilled his coffee cup and set it on the battered wooden table. He was in the mood for a fight and hoped his visitor was in the mood to accommodate him. His crappy frame of mind was directly linked to the absence of sunshine in his life. He missed Sam. It was as simple and as complicated as that. She was his sunshine and without her he was a storm waiting to happen. But he managed to taint everyone he touched and he just couldn't do that to her.

When the door opened again, Connor Ryan stood there with an armed and dangerous expression on his face. But Mitch's first thought was that something was wrong.

"Is Sam okay?"

"She's fine."

"So what brings you here?"

"Sam."

Mitch braced his feet wide apart and crossed his arms over his chest. "So Rhonda was right. You are the official type. Authorized spokesperson for the Ryan family."

"No one sent me." A muscle in Connor's jaw jerked. "Including my sister."

"Oh?"

"In fact, she made me promise not to make things worse by confronting you."

Mitch looked him over. "Since you're here, you obviously take after your mother."

"I only promised not to make her life more complicated."

"Do you have a plan for that?"

"Always," Connor answered.

There was a protectiveness in his stance that bothered Mitch. How stupid was that? The guy was there to look after his sister, see to her welfare. It was a job Mitch wanted but had no right to do and every reason not to if he was going to safeguard her best interests. And he couldn't help being ticked off that he wasn't Sam's go-to guy.

"Are you going to share this plan?" Mitch didn't even try to take the edge off his irritation.

"There's nothing to share. I want to know what your intentions are toward my sister."

Mitch slid his hands into the pockets of his lab coat and curled his fingers into fists. "So you're like your father after all."

"I'll take that as a compliment since it's obvious that my dad already asked you the same question."

"He did."

Connor's eyes narrowed. "And what was the answer?"

"I told him I'd never do anything to hurt Sam."

"Then you've already failed miserably."

Anger exploded through him and Mitch took a step forward. "What the hell does that mean?"

"It means that I held my sister while she cried and you're the guy responsible."

Sam was crying? Damn it. "I haven't even seen her—"

"Bingo," he said, pointing an accusing finger.

"It's for her own good."

"She's pregnant. With your baby. How do you figure it's best to abandon her?"

Mitch winced at his choice of words. If he wasn't so angry, probably he'd be more inclined to see another point of view. But right now he didn't give a damn about being a bridge or getting past obstacles. His goal was to keep Sam from being hurt and taking himself out of the equation was the best way to do that.

"I want what's best for Sam."

"You've got a funny way of showing it," Connor said.

"Yeah, well, I've got my reasons. You'll just have to take my word on that."

"This is my sister and her baby. Where her welfare is concerned, your word's not good enough."

Mitch dragged his fingers through his hair. "It's all I've got. My word and a relationship track record littered with casualties. I don't want to do that to Sam."

"Have you considered what she wants?"

"Of course I have. Her happiness and the baby's are my primary concern."

"Again I have to say that disappearing without a word is a funny way of showing that."

"Look, Connor," he said, the anger suddenly draining out of him. "I care about Sam more than I've ever cared about anyone in my life. I know my word doesn't have much capital with you, but that's the God's honest truth."

"Right." Sarcasm dripped off the single word.

"Believe it." He shrugged. "Or not. There's nothing I can do about that. But Sam and the baby won't want for anything. Not ever."

"Except for your emotional support."

"You couldn't be more wrong."

"So you love my sister?"

God, yes, he wanted to shout. He loved her with everything he had. He loved her enough to let her go. He loved her enough not to discuss it with her brother. "It's none of your business."

"But you care?"

"Of course I do. The day she was here and I didn't know if I was going to lose her, or the baby, or both—" He dragged in a long breath. "I've had some days that really sucked. But that day, before I knew she was stable, that day was the worst."

"Have you told her how you feel?" Connor demanded.

Mitch stared at the other man for several moments. "I thought you promised not to make her life more complicated."

"I did. This should simplify everything."

"What the hell are you talking about? What do you want from me?"

"I'll tell you what I want." Connor took a step forward. "Put up or shut up. Quit trying to look like a hero instead of the coward you obviously are. You're trying to play both sides of the fence and it's not going to work. Either have the decency to tell Sam you love her or tell her that you're just not into her. But for God's sake face her. Then get the hell out of her life."

They stared at each other for several moments, both breathing hard as if punches had been thrown. Mitch wanted to hit something, but if Sam had taught him anything it was to think first. And before he could come back with any kind of retort, Connor had turned away and walked out, his angry words hanging in the air.

Get the hell out of her life.

More than once within the walls of Mercy Medical Center Mitch had battled death to preserve a life. He'd faced worried family members with good news and bad and always told it like it was, straightforward truth. That wasn't always easy. Somewhere along the line he'd lost himself. He'd been punishing himself for not being able to save Robbie or his marriage. He'd resigned himself to being alone. And he had been.

Until Sam had marched into his E.R. to do battle for his soul.

Now he couldn't picture his world without her in it. If there was no one to care about, no one you couldn't wait to see at the end of a long day, no one who cared whether or not you came home at all, what did any of it mean?

Mitch realized he couldn't get the hell out of Sam's life.

She *was* his life.

In Darlyn's office, Sam sat down across the desk from her boss. "Thanks for making time to see me."

"No problem." Darlyn rested her glasses on top of her short, auburn hair. "What's up?"

She folded her hands in her lap and decided not to beat around the bush. Straight out. No introduction or sugarcoating. "I'm pregnant."

"Wow." Warm brown eyes went from shock to sympathy to sheer delight. As she continued to observe, an assessing expression settled on her face. "Are congratulations in order?"

"Yes—if morning sickness and feeling like roadkill are cause for celebration."

"I want to know how you feel about this, Sam. I'm your friend as well as your boss and I can support this in whatever way you need."

"I want this child very much."

"That's what I wanted to hear." Darlyn grinned. "My gosh, a baby."

"Yeah."

"Is the father happy, too?"

"I don't think so."

"Did he say so?"

"Not in so many words. But actions speak louder." Sam gripped her hands so tightly they hurt. Maybe that would take the edge off how she hurt inside.

"Do you want me to take a whack at him?"

One corner of Sam's mouth turned up. "My brother already offered."

"You're not going to throw me a bone, are you? You're going to make me ask who he is."

"I'm not going to make you do anything."

"Mitch Tenney is the father, isn't he?"

Sam was too surprised to sidestep the question. "How did you know?"

"I was guessing, but you just confirmed." Darlyn nodded with satisfaction. "Don't ever give up your day job to play poker. You don't know the first thing about bluffing."

"But what made you think of him?"

"Three things," she said holding up one finger. "He switched coaches twice. The first time because you intrigued him, the second because you two were involved. I knew he pushed your buttons when you were reluctant to take him on as a client, but I thought they were professional ones."

"It's complicated. I just thought you should know about the baby. If you want my resignation—"

"No way." Darlyn held up her hand. "After getting that new corporate contract I need you more than ever. You wouldn't abandon me now."

"Not if you want me."

"You're very good at what you do and I absolutely would like you to stay on. We can work out the details of your maternity leave as your due date gets closer."

Sam breathed a sigh of relief. "Thank you. That's a load off my mind."

"We can set up on site day care," her boss said. "I know some people at UNLV's early childhood development program. Maybe I can work out an internship situation with the students."

One of Sam's major concerns was financial, and keeping her job was crucial. She'd never expected this kind of support, too. She knew that if her mother had been there, this was how she'd have reacted. Her throat thick with emotion, Sam could only nod.

Everything was falling into place, everything but Mitch.

Darlyn looked at the watch on her wrist. "I have someone coming in now. If you need to talk more I can—"

Sam shook her head and stood. "It's fine. I just wanted to tell you what was going on."

"If you need anything, don't hesitate to ask. I'm throwing a baby shower."

At the door Sam rested her hand on the knob. "You're going to arm wrestle my sister Fiona for that right. And I should warn you, she might look delicate, but she's got some moves."

Darlyn laughed. "We'll work something out. I can hardly wait. See you later."

Sam nodded, then left the office. She stopped in the bathroom before going back to her own space. Skidding to a stop in the doorway, she saw Mitch standing in front of her desk.

"Hi," he said, lifting his hand in a wave.

"What are you doing here?"

"That gave me a warm fuzzy."

She was warm, too, and fuzzy had nothing to do with it. Her heart was beating fast, probably because she was so glad to see him. When her brain took over she'd be all right.

"I haven't seen you for several weeks. It's a logical question," she said, proud of the coolness in her tone.

That was when she saw the cellophane-wrapped bouquet of flowers on her desk. She met his gaze and her pulse kicked up again. "Tell me those aren't for me."

He slid his hands into the pockets of his battered brown leather jacket. "I could do that, but it would be a lie."

"That's out of character for you."

"Not anymore," he said. "Coaching has made a new man of me."

Sam so didn't need this. Most of the time she felt like she wanted to throw up and today was no exception. Definitely she wasn't at her best. Then he shows up looking like Hollywood's hunk of the hour just when she was getting a handle on how to move forward without him. It wasn't fair. On top of that, it was breaking her heart.

"I'm very glad you've benefited from the Marshall Management program. Your continued success is thanks enough," she said, looking at the gorgeous roses. "Now, if you'll excuse me, I have a client coming."

Not until after lunch, but he didn't need to know that.

"You're throwing me out?"

"Yes."

"Déjà vu all over again," he said.

"What does that mean?"

"The very first time I was here you told me we wouldn't be a good fit. As it turned out, we fit together very well."

His voice dropped into the seductive range that never failed to start flutters deep inside her. "Look, Mitch, on a professional level, I'm very happy that your work issues have been resolved. I don't think there's anything left to say—"

"I do. And I bought three sessions of your donated time at the fund-raiser. I can dig out the voucher, if you don't remember—"

"I do." She'd never forgotten. It was the night she fell in love with him, the same night their baby was conceived. "We can schedule time, just see the receptionist on your way out."

"There's no time like the present. Your next client can just wait." He moved closer. "No one knows better than me that you're worth waiting for."

"I don't understand." Sam took a step back and felt her desk behind her. "What is this?"

"This is me trying to apologize for being an ass."

"Why?"

"I love you. I want to marry you."

Shock didn't come close to how she felt. This was a declaration she'd never expected to hear from Mitch Tenney. "Is that so?" was all she could manage to say.

"Yes." His gaze narrowed even as a glint of something sharpened in his blue eyes. "Do you have a problem with that?"

"As a matter of fact—" She nodded. "It's hard for me to believe since you have an irrational fear of being responsible for someone else's destiny."

"I see." He nodded thoughtfully as he moved even closer. "Is there anything else you think I need to know?"

"Now that you mention it." She tried to shrink away from him but there was nowhere to go. Resting her hand behind her, she felt the smooth cellophane surrounding the roses. "If this is a pity proposal, you can save your breath. My father and I had a long talk and were able to smooth out the issues between us. My family is behind me one hundred percent, as is my boss. So I'm not alone. The baby and I will be fine."

"Good to know." Nodding, he slid a finger softly, gently down her cheek. "You're certain that it's in the best interests of you and the baby to be on your own?"

"It's not ideal, but that pretty well describes life in general. We'll be fine. Don't worry about us—"

"What if I can't help it?"

"That's not something I can do anything about."

"What if you could do something?"

She stared at him. This was Mitch, but different. He was the same unyielding man, but he wasn't being oppositional or defiant. The intense, argumentative doctor she'd first known was gone. In his place was a man who was... Asking questions in order to turn her views to his way of thinking.

"You're using my techniques against me," she accused.

He had the audacity to grin. "I'm a quick learner."

"There's more to a relationship than conflict resolution. Why the sudden change of heart?"

"Something your brother said." The smile disappeared, replaced by an impassioned expression that was new.

"Connor went to see you?"

"Yeah. And it has to be said that he could benefit from your coaching." He ran his fingers through his hair. "But he was right about one thing."

"What?" she whispered.

"He told me that I should either tell you I love you or get the hell out of your life. I can't do that, the second one. It's safe to say that I don't suffer fools easily. And he made me realize that it would be foolish to throw away the best thing that's ever happened to me."

This was a lot to take in. "You mean me?"

"Yes." He cupped her face in his warm hands and looked into her eyes. "It wouldn't be smart to let your pride get in the way of what we have. If I could figure out how to make this a question, I would. But I can't so I'll just say it straight out. When you love someone being responsible isn't a burden. It's a joy. You're not alone, Sam. As long as there's breath in my body you'll never be alone again."

Her gaze slid over his face, the intensity she'd admired and been drawn to right from the first. This straightforward Mitch was like the man she'd fallen in live with, but different, too. He was more lighthearted and tender.

"I'm afraid to believe."

"I'll see your fear and raise you a terror or two." He brushed his thumb over her bottom lip. "I'm more afraid of being without you than you could ever be of anything. You're my bridge and we're the right people. If we're together, there's nothing but opportunity for happiness." He let out a long breath. "I understand your hesitation. I can respect it, but walking away is not an option. I'll keep coming back until I wear down your resistance. I'll be here until you get that I'm not going away and you, of all people, know how stubborn I am. I love you, Sam. I want to spend the rest of my life with you. Marry me. Please."

He'd had her from that very first time she'd seen him go to battle for a little boy's life. He didn't give up and he didn't censor his words when he cared passionately.

He was right. It wasn't very bright to throw away what you wanted most when it was right there for the taking.

Sam smiled up at him as happiness poured through her. "I've been in love with you from the first moment I saw you in action in Mercy Medical's E.R. You're my hero, Mitch. There's nothing that would make me happier than being your wife and raising our child with you."

He smiled, then kissed her softly before pulling her into his arms where she felt safe. "I'm thinking a Christmas wedding. What do you think, Sunshine?"

"Perfect."

And it was. This was everything she'd always wanted—to love and be hopelessly in love with Mitch Tenney. She was expecting the doctor's baby.

Life didn't get any more perfect.

* * * * *

Turn the page for a sneak preview of AFTERSHOCK,
a new anthology featuring New York Times
bestselling author Sharon Sala.

Available October 2008.

n⬤cturne™

*Dramatic and sensual tales
of paranormal romance.*

Chapter 1

October
New York City

Nicole Masters was sitting cross-legged on her sofa while a cold autumn rain peppered the windows of her fourth-floor apartment. She was poking at the ice cream in her bowl and trying not to be in a mood.

Six weeks ago, a simple trip to her neighborhood pharmacy had turned into a nightmare. She'd walked into the middle of a robbery. She never even saw the man who shot her in the head and left her for dead. She'd survived, but some of her senses had not. She was dealing with short-term memory loss and a tendency to stagger. Even though she'd been told the problems were most likely temporary, she waged a daily battle with depression.

Her parents had been killed in a car wreck when she was twenty-one. And except for a few friends—and most recently her boyfriend, Dominic Tucci, who lived in the apartment right above hers, she was alone. Her doctor kept reminding her that she should be grateful to be alive, and on one level she knew he was right. But he wasn't living in her shoes.

If she'd been anywhere else but at that pharmacy when the robbery happened, she wouldn't have died twice on the way to the hospital. Instead of being grateful that she'd survived, she couldn't stop thinking of what she'd lost.

But that wasn't the end of her troubles. On top of everything else, something strange was happening inside her head. She'd begun to hear odd things: sounds, not voices—at least, she didn't think it was voices. It was more like the distant noise of rapids—a rush of wind and water inside her head that, when it came, blocked out everything around her. It didn't happen often, but when it did, it was frightening, and it was driving her crazy.

The blank moments, which is what she called them, even had a rhythm. First there came that sound, then a cold sweat, then panic with no reason. Part of her feared it was the beginning of an emotional breakdown. And part of her feared it wasn't—that it was going to turn out to be a permanent souvenir of her resurrection.

Frustrated with herself and the situation as it stood, she upped the sound on the TV remote. But instead of *Wheel of Fortune*, an announcer broke in with a special bulletin.

"This just in. Police are on the scene of a kidnapping that occurred only hours ago at The Dakota. Molly Dane, the six-year-old daughter of one of Hollywood's block-buster stars, Lyla Dane, was taken by force from the family apartment. At this time they have yet to receive a ransom demand. The housekeeper was seriously injured during the abduction, and is, at the present time, in surgery. Police are hoping to be able to talk to her once she regains consciousness. In the meantime, we are going now to a press conference with Lyla Dane."

Horrified, Nicole stilled as the cameras went live to where the actress was speaking before a bank of microphones. The shock and terror in Lyla Dane's voice were physically painful to watch. But even though Nicole kept upping the volume, the sound continued to fade.

Just when she was beginning to think something was wrong with her set, the broadcast suddenly switched from the Dane press conference to what appeared to be footage of the kidnapping, beginning with footage from inside the apartment.

When the front door suddenly flew back against the wall and four men rushed in, Nicole gasped. Horrified, she quickly realized that this must have been caught on a security camera inside the Dane apartment.

As Nicole continued to watch, a small Asian woman, who she guessed was the maid, rushed forward in an effort to keep them out. When one of the men hit her in the face with his gun, Nicole moaned. The violence was too reminiscent of what she'd lived through. Sick to her stomach, she fisted her hands against her belly, wishing it was over, but unable to tear her gaze away.

When the maid dropped to the carpet, the same man followed with a vicious kick to the little woman's midsection that lifted her off the floor.

"Oh, my God," Nicole said. When blood began to pool beneath the maid's head, she started to cry.

As the tape played on, the four men split up in different directions. The camera caught one running down a long marble hallway, then disappearing into a room. Moments later he reappeared, carrying a little girl, who Nicole assumed was Molly Dane. The child was wearing a pair of red pants and a white turtleneck sweater, and her hair was partially blocking her abductor's face as he carried her down the hall. She was kicking and screaming in his arms, and when he slapped her, it elicited an agonized scream that brought the other three running. Nicole watched in horror as one of them ran up and put his hand over Molly's face. Seconds later, she went limp.

One moment they were in the foyer, then they were gone.

Nicole jumped to her feet, then staggered drunkenly. The bowl of ice cream she'd absentmindedly placed in her lap shattered at her feet, splattering glass and melting ice cream everywhere.

The picture on the screen abruptly switched from the kidnapping to what Nicole assumed was a rerun of Lyla Dane's plea for her daughter's safe return, but she was numb.

Before she could think what to do next, the doorbell rang. Startled by the unexpected sound, she shakily swiped at the tears and took a step forward. She didn't feel the glass shards piercing her feet until she took the second step. At that point, sharp pains shot through her foot. She gasped, then looked down in confusion. Her legs looked as if she'd been running through mud, and she was standing in broken glass and ice cream, while a thin ribbon of blood seeped out from beneath her toes.

"Oh, no," Nicole mumbled, then stifled a second moan of pain.

The doorbell rang again. She shivered, then clutched her head in confusion.

"Just a minute!" she yelled, then tried to sidestep the rest of the debris as she hobbled to the door.

When she looked through the peephole in the door, she didn't know whether to be relieved or regretful.

It was Dominic, and as usual, she was a mess.

Nicole smiled a little self-consciously as she opened the door to let him in. "I just don't know what's happening to me. I think I'm losing my mind."

"Hey, don't talk about my woman like that."

Nicole rode the surge of delight his words brought. "So I'm still your woman?"

Dominic lowered his head.

Their lips met.

The kiss proceeded.

Slowly.

Thoroughly.

* * * * *

Be sure to look for the
AFTERSHOCK
anthology next month, as well as
other exciting paranormal stories
from Silhouette Nocturne.
Available in October wherever books are sold.